D1095634

A HOUSE IN THE UPLANDS

BOOKS BY ERSKINE CALDWELL

Novels

TOBACCO ROAD
GOD'S LITTLE ACRE
JOURNEYMAN
TROUBLE IN JULY
ALL NIGHT LONG
GEORGIA BOY
TRAGIC GROUND
A HOUSE IN THE UPLANDS

Volumes of Short Stories

AMERICAN EARTH
WE ARE THE LIVING
KNEEL TO THE RISING SUN
SOUTHWAYS
JACKPOT
STORIES

Social Studies

SOME AMERICAN PEOPLE
YOU HAVE SEEN THEIR FACES
  (*with Margaret Bourke-White*)

Travel

NORTH OF THE DANUBE
  (*with Margaret Bourke-White*)
SAY! IS THIS THE U. S. A.
  (*with Margaret Bourke-White*)

War Correspondence

ALL-OUT ON THE ROAD TO SMOLENSK
MOSCOW UNDER FIRE
RUSSIA AT WAR
  (*with Margaret Bourke-White*)

A HOUSE IN
THE UPLANDS

BY

ERSKINE CALDWELL

NEW YORK

DUELL, SLOAN AND PEARCE

FOR JAY

A HOUSE IN THE UPLANDS

Chapter I

A SOUTHERLY BREEZE FROM the low country, languid and moist, was drifting over the newly plowed fields of the upland slope and rustling the leaves of the tall red oaks that surrounded the aging house. It was twilight in the early spring. The nightbirds, having roosted silently in the trees through the heat of the day, were fluttering restlessly. Now that the birds were awake, they would chirp shrilly until dawn.

At the bottom of the slope, half a mile away, a blue haze of woodsmoke floated in a thin wafer of a cloud above a groundfire in a patch of pines that had been burning wild and untended for several days. From time to time there was a sudden bright flare of yellowish flame when a turpentine cup on a tree was ignited by the creeping groundfire.

Southward to the coast lay the low country, a flat sparsely settled expanse of moss-draped cypress, stagnant pools of ground water, and silent green glades. To the west of the groundfire, for mile after mile, dense dark piney woods were spread like a wrinkled carpet upon the undulating land, and to the east of it, the muddy yellow river flowed tirelessly to the sea. The gully-washed red clay hills, jagged and lacerated, scalloped the pale Piedmont sky in the north.

Lucyanne heard Martha's ponderous bare feet plodding across the veranda, and a moment later Martha, exceedingly black and fleshy, was standing beside her chair.

"What is it, Martha?" she asked without looking up.

Martha, heaving her heavy breasts and sighing dolefully, shifted the weight of her body from one foot to the other. She was good-natured and understanding, often to an irritating extent, and easily moved to tears. Seemingly at will, streams of tears would flow effortlessly and copiously down her gleaming black cheeks. She was somewhere between fifty and sixty years old and had lived at one time or another, under the common law, with half a dozen men. At the moment she was without a man and, curiously, proudly bemoaned the fact that she was a green grass widow at her age.

"What do you want, Martha?" Lucyanne asked, annoyed by her silence.

"I thought maybe you might want me to sit and miserate with you a little bit, Miss Lucyanne. It sure does look like Mr. Grady ain't going to come home in time for his supper again." As a token of her sympathy, she sighed mournfully. "Oh me my! Looks like he'd done gone and been here by now, iffen he was coming at all, don't it, Miss Lucyanne?"

Lucyanne closed her eyes tightly for a moment before she could bring herself to answer Martha. When she opened them again, she could see Martha's huge body swaying rhythmically, each motion accompanied by a deep and sorrowing moan.

"I don't know," she said, keeping her voice even and controlled. "It's early yet, Martha."

"It ain't never too early for a man to come home." There was a moment's pause. "Specially a married man."

Lucyanne made no reply, and Martha sighed deeply again, anxious to let her commiseration be known.

"Well, I done finished up in the kitchen, and I reckon I could put Mr. Grady's supper on the cookstove where it'll stay partly warm for a little while, iffen the stovewood don't go and burn out too fast, and iffen he comes home tonight at all. I just don't never know what to do exactly about Mr. Grady," she said, her words trailing off into an indistinct and irritating mumble.

"That'll be all right, Martha," she spoke up hastily, hoping the tone of her voice would indicate that she wanted Martha to go away and leave her alone. Martha, however, made no move to leave. "You can go now," she added firmly.

"Yessum," Martha said uneasily.

She still did not leave, though, and Lucyanne looked up at her impatiently. Martha's lips were beginning to quiver as they always did when she was getting ready to cry. She fidgeted for a moment, and then a stream of tears began flowing down each black cheek.

"Miss Lucyanne, maybe iff   you gets too awful lonesome to stand it all by yourself I could stay and sort of keep you company for a little while." She wailed, unrestrained. "I know how it is to have a man be off somewhere else in the night time when he ain't got no business doing it. It's just like not having no man at all, only it's a heap worse because you've got him but you ain't." She wailed plaintively. "It sure looks like Mr. Grady ain't coming home tonight again, and it

don't help none at all for you to stay by yourself
all the time. I'll just sit and keep you company and
tell you about the hard life I've led with menfolks in my time," she said, her words once more
becoming indistinct and mumbly.

"I'll be all right, Martha," she said sharply.
"You can go home now."

"Yessum," Martha replied without conviction.

She waited for Martha to leave, wanting more
than ever to be alone. Martha shifted the weight
of her body again and sighed sympathetically.
The tears continued to flow down her cheeks.

"Miss Lucyanne?" she murmured with a sob.

"What is it, Martha?"

"What in the world you reckon Mr. Grady does
all the time when he's gone away like this? Don't
he never tell you nothing when he comes back?
Reckon he messes around with some lady friend
like he oughtn't? Oh me my! I declare, menfolks
sure can be the hardest people in the world to get
along with, somehow."

Her body shook with wails of grief as she
stopped and dabbed at her cheeks with the corner of her apron.

"Miss Lucyanne, you sure ought to speak up
and say something to Mr. Grady about his going
on. Iffen I had a man who stayed out like that, I'd
speak my piece to him, and I wouldn't take no

uppance from him, neither. That's the only way in this big wide world to make a man behave himself. Now you know as well as I do that there ain't a bit of sense going to all the trouble of getting a man iffen he ain't never at home to do the dutiful thing." She sighed deeply. "Ain't nothing in the world can take the place of a good man doing the dutiful thing at the right time in the right place."

"That's enough!" Lucyanne said sharply. "I don't want to hear another word of that kind of talk, Martha!"

"Yessum," she murmured sorrowfully.

"Go on home now, Martha."

"Yessum," she said, drying her eyes with her apron.

After releasing a parting convulsive sob, Martha waddled across the veranda and into the house. When she was certain Martha had left, Lucyanne closed her eyes wearily and listened to the chirping of the nightbirds. The evening breeze from the low country, rising gently, blew against her feverish skin as she sat still and quiet in the long spring twilight. After a few minutes she got up and walked restlessly back and forth on the veranda. She did not know how she could ever make herself become accustomed to waiting patiently for Grady to come home. It seemed to her then that her whole life had been spent in the silent barn-like house wondering where he was, what he was doing, and when he would come back.

Presently she heard the tapping of a cane on the veranda, and Mama Elsie, Grady's mother, walked laboriously from the door to her rocker. Mama Elsie was a large heavy woman in her seventies who had grown to be quarrelsome and carping. Grady was her only child, and she made no attempt to hide her resentment of Lucyanne. In fact, Lucyanne knew that she went out of her way at every opportunity to make life as unpleasant as possible. After almost a whole year she still treated Lucyanne like a stranger and an outsider.

Lucyanne went to her chair and sat down.

Mama Elsie rocked back and forth several times before speaking. The monotonous squeaking of the rocking chair at a time like that always seemed to Lucyanne to be the inevitable tuning for her whining voice.

"What on earth were you doing when I came out here, child?" she began in her domineering manner. "Why were you pacing up and down like a caged animal?"

"I'm waiting for Grady, Mama Elsie," she replied, frightened and trembling. "I was hoping he'd come home tonight."

"God have mercy on me," Mama Elsie said. "I never thought I'd be forced to spend my declining years in the same house, and in my own house at that, with a creature who carries on the way you do. You sit here and mope like this day after day without end. You are spite and determined to make my son's life miserable for him."

"No, Mama Elsie! You don't understand!"

"I don't, huh? Well, I'm no fool. I know what you're after. You want Grady to lie at your feet day and night like a common dog. Grady's entitled to any and all freedom he wishes. When he's ready to come home, he'll come home. You're making a fool of yourself behaving the way you do. God have mercy on me, I hope he never lets himself be cowed and browbeaten into doing anything he doesn't want to do. It would be an everlasting shame if he thought he had to live his life the way you want him to live it. God have mercy on me."

Lucyanne bit her lips, reminding herself how useless it was to try to defend herself at a time like that. She closed her eyes, hoping the silence, this time at least, would discourage Mama Elsie from going into one of her seemingly endless tirades. Above the sound of the squeaking chair, the noisy chirping of the nightbirds was soothing and restful.

Nothing was said for several minutes, and the squeaking ceased abruptly.

"I hear a car coming up the lane," Mama Elsie said, startling her. "It's probably Grady."

Lucyanne jumped up immediately and ran to the veranda railing. An automobile, partly obscured by the leafy trees, actually was coming up the lane. She leaned forward, gripping the railing tensely.

"See?" Mama Elsie said in her provoking manner, rocking her chair triumphantly. "I told you Grady would be coming home when he was ready, didn't I? Now, maybe you can see what a fool you've made of yourself. Next time see if you can control yourself in a more respectable manner."

Lucyanne smoothed her dress and touched her hair with shaking fingers. The car was turning into the driveway.

"Now, whatever you do, don't go and forget yourself in Grady's presence," she continued garrulously. "Remember who you are. I'd rather be dead in my grave than to see my son afflicted with the kind of wife who nags him about where he's been and what he's been doing every minute while he's been away. God have mercy on me. And next time don't make a fool of yourself when he stays away a few days. He'll always come home when he's ready to come. Grady is entitled to certain privileges you have no right to question. Apparently that is something you have never learned. God have mercy on me."

"It's Grady—it's him!" she said excitedly.

"You'd better learn to pay attention to what I tell you, young lady," Mama Elsie said, "because as long as I draw the breath of life I'm going to see to it that Grady isn't made miserable by somebody he should never have married in the first place."

Chapter II

THE HEAVY COUPE STOPPED under the vine-covered portico at the side of the house, the sudden locking of brakes rocking it from end to end. Grinning broadly, Grady sat still for several moments. Then with slow and deliberate movements he opened the door and dropped his feet to the ground. Shoving himself from the car, he moved unsteadily towards the veranda steps. He had not shaved for three days, and his thick black hair was tousled and uncombed. His shirt tail was hanging out and he had left his necktie somewhere. Dried red mud was caked on his shoes. He looked as though he had not slept for several nights. However, he was still boyish and handsome in appearance. He was unusually tall and slender with dark, almost Negroid, complexion.

Joyfully, Lucyanne ran down the steps to meet

him. When he saw her, and recognized who she was, he stopped and took several steps backward. There he gazed at her appraisingly, watching the youthful and graceful movements of her body as though he had forgotten completely what she really looked like. He cocked his head to one side and nodded approvingly.

"Oh, Grady!" she cried, going towards him.

"Stay where you are!" he called out in an unusually loud voice, at the same time waving her away with an unsteady motion of his hands.

She stopped where she was, wondering, but smiling at him with delight.

"I'm so glad to see you, Grady!" she said eagerly. "I missed you so much!"

He took a step sideways and surveyed her from head to toe.

"I'm awfully glad you're back, Grady."

"A well-spoken greeting, Lucyannie. Couldn't ask for a better one. Very, very befitting."

"You know I mean it, don't you, Grady?"

"Of course you do, Lucyannie. Of course you do."

Each time he came home after an absence of several days he was immediately and completely fascinated by the sight of her but, invariably, after a few minutes he apparently lost all interest in her. Each time it happened, Lucyanne tried to conceal her disappointment and hoped that next time would be different. Now she felt like crying when she saw the smile leave his face. In an effort to hide her feelings, she ran down the steps. He put out his arms to hug her, but in doing so he lost his balance and would have fallen if she had not caught him.

"Oh, Grady, you're drunk," she said unhappily. She realized at once that she should not have said it, but it was too late.

"That's my business, and I've got plenty of it," he said roughly, scowling at her. After that he shook himself free. "I attend to my business, you attend to yours."

"I'm sorry I said that, Grady," she said desperately. "I didn't mean it—it doesn't matter!"

He leaned against her clumsily, lightly kissing her cheek. She had never been able to resist him when he kissed her or put his arms around her, and now more than ever she felt drawn to him. She found his hand and squeezed it eagerly.

"No hard feelings, are there, Lucyannie?" he said, his boyish smile driving all anger from her. She was so glad to have him back that his drunkenness no longer made any difference to her. "What do you say, Lucyannie?"

"Of course not, Grady," she told him quickly, pressing herself tightly in his arms.

"Fine and dandy," he said, roughly pushing her away.

She reached for his hand and tried to lead him towards the steps. He jerked his hand from hers.

"Let's go in the house, Grady," she urged, "and I'll get you some clean clothes." She looked into his eyes appealingly. "You can shave and take a shower, and when you've finished, I'll have everything ready for you. Wouldn't you like to do that, Grady? Please, Grady!"

He slapped at her, knocking her hand away.

"Oh, no you don't, smarty!" he said loudly, continuing to slap at her. "I know what you're after. You can't fool me. You're trying to get me in there so you can bawl hell out of me for staying away three days and coming home looking like a—like a what? What do I look like, Lucyannie?"

"Grady, you know that's not true," she protested. "I've never done such a thing. I'm not angry—I'm too glad to see you to be angry. Please don't say that."

"I'll say what I please, Lucyannie."

"But that's unfair, Grady. I've never tried to trick you like that."

"I'm playing safe, just the same," he told her as he went past her up the steps. "You stay out here."

She followed him across the veranda.

"Please let me come, Grady," she begged unashamedly. "I want to be with you."

"Shut up and do like I tell you," he said meanly, turning and glaring at her. "I don't want to have to tell you more than once, either."

Lucyanne could see Mama Elsie smiling to herself as she moved back and forth in her squeaking chair. As he passed his mother, Grady patted her briefly on the shoulder. Mama Elsie turned her head and watched him approvingly as he went to the front door.

Still hopeful that he would change his mind, Lucyanne followed him almost to the door before he turned and saw her.

"I'll give you one more chance to do what I told you," he warned her.

He stumbled through the door and went into the hall.

"Lucyanne!" Mama Elsie said in a loud voice. "Come back here!"

She hesitated, wanting more than anything else in the world to be allowed to go to Grady's room with him. She listened to his heavy stumbling tread on the stairway.

"Come here before you make a bigger fool of yourself," Mama Elsie said sharply. "God have mercy on me."

~ 17 ~

She turned and walked slowly to the chair she had been sitting in when Grady came.

"I hope I never live to see such a disgusting spectacle again in this house," she began, her cold gaze fixed upon Lucyanne. "If you never do anything else as long as you live in this house, you've got to learn to listen to what Grady tells you to do. The men of the family have always been the masters of the house. It's a disgrace to see your kind of behavior."

Lucyanne, with tears welling in her eyes, cried brokenly. Mama Elsie, resuming her rocking in the squeaky chair, watched her dispassionately.

"Have yourself a good cry," she said, smiling contentedly, "and maybe you'll get that unforgivable streak out of your nature. Anyway, crying is good for you at a time like this. Some of these days you'll learn to do what Grady tells you to do and stop making these disgusting scenes. Dunbar women have always obeyed. You will, too."

"But it's so senseless, Mama Elsie," she protested helplessly. "And I don't care what anybody else has ever done. I don't like to be treated like a—like a—I don't know what! It's not decent—it's not right!"

"God have mercy on me. That has nothing to do with it. It's the Dunbar tradition, child. You were an outsider. You married into the family, and it's up to you to learn to adjust yourself to our way of living. Besides, you brought all this on yourself when you married Grady. Now make the best of it."

"But Grady gets worse all the time, Mama Elsie. He needs somebody to make him stop what he's doing."

"When you contrived in your foxy way to marry my son, was it your idea that you were going to change him? Was that your reason for marrying him? To make him over according to your notion of what a man should be? God have mercy on me."

"Of course not," she said. "I didn't think anything like that. But I did think Grady would be different after we were married."

She could hear Grady's mother chuckling to herself.

"It'll never be different, child," she said after a while. "You might as well save yourself a world of grief and make up your mind to that now as later. I learned my lesson when I married Grady's father. He was just like Grady. He refused to be dominated by a woman. It took me almost forty years of living with him to become resigned to that fact. Some day you'll learn what all the women of the family have learned. A Dunbar is a Dunbar, and nobody's going to change him."

"But Grady is so willful and headstrong about everything, Mama Elsie. He won't listen to me at all. And you take up for him every time, no matter what he says or does. That's what makes everything so difficult."

"God have mercy on me. The men of the family have always had the say-so about the way we live, and it doesn't sound any too good to have a somebody who merely married into the family criticize and find fault with us. We don't need advice from outsiders. We are as good as any family that ever walked this earth, and if you're determined to stay here, you'll have to learn to be like us. You talk like some foreigner who has no respect whatever for our traditions, but I suppose that's to be expected of someone with no background and with no family connections with anybody I ever heard of. It's a shame the way awful people are moving into our part of the country from the outside and trying to mingle with us on our own level. Nobody knows a thing about your family's background. They've lived here for only ten years. No, you're far from being entitled to enjoy the privileges of being one us."

"That's exactly how I feel!" Lucyanne said.

"God have mercy on me. I knew it—I knew it! God is punishing us for Grady's moment of weakness, but it's you who should be punished for entangling Grady with your female wiles. If his father had been alive, he'd have bought you off and saved us this disgrace. Every time my boy went to Atlanta or Savannah I feared he'd be snared by somebody like you, somebody he only wanted for a plaything for a few days. I knew the first time I laid eyes on you that you were going to be the ruination of this family. It's all part and parcel of your diabolical scheme."

"I don't know what you mean! What are you talking about?"

"It's as plain as broad daylight that you're scheming to let the Dunbar name die out——"

"But it's not my fault, Mama Elsie. If you would try——"

"I can draw my own conclusions, young woman."

"Please believe me, Mama Elsie. It's Grady who——"

"God have mercy on me. That's a deliberate falsehood, and you know it's a lie!" She was shaking with anger. "The idea! You trying to blame my son for your own shortcomings and deceit! I won't listen to a word of it! It's ridiculous—it's downright absurd! The idea! I wish Grady could hear you talk like that—he'd soon put an end to it!"

"But if Grady would only——"

"There's plenty of manhood left in this family, if that's what you're hinting at, young lady," she stated with elaborate inflection. "It's womanhood that's lacking in this house now." She regarded Lucyanne with a haughty and superior stare. "The idea!"

Lucyanne buried her face in her hands and wept. Each time she had attempted to tell Mama Elsie what the trouble was, Mama Elsie refused to listen to her. She had chided Lucyanne incessantly all winter and spring, and Lucyanne had grown to dread being in her presence.

"That won't help matters one bit," Mama Elsie said unfeelingly. "Save your weeping to use on a man. A woman is too accustomed to tears to have any regard for them."

"But Grady just doesn't—he doesn't do anything about it, Mama Elsie," she said in a desperate effort to convince her. "You've got to believe me!"

"God have mercy on me," she said. "I won't sit here and listen to such talk about my son, even if you do pretend to be his wife."

"But it's true, whether you want to believe it or not," she said calmly.

"I'll never believe a word you say after this if you persist in saying such things about my son," she said, getting up from her chair and moving past Lucyanne. "I've always suspected that you were irresponsible and untrustworthy, and now this proves it once and for all. You are an utterly shameless creature, blaming your shortcomings on poor Grady. It's a pity he allowed himself to be caught in your clutches. My heart bleeds for the poor boy. God have mercy on me."

She left Lucyanne crying in the darkness.

Chapter III

Lucyanne had waited as long as she could before leaving the veranda and going into the house. It was completely dark by then and no lights had been turned on.

Feeling her way through the inky darkness of the hall she hurried up the stairway to the second floor. She paused for a moment to get her breath back and then, treading lightly, went past Grady's door on her way to her own room. She wanted to burst into his room and throw herself into his arms, but she forced herself to keep on walking down the hall, carefully avoiding the squeaky flooring so Grady would not know she had come upstairs. He had told her to stay on the veranda, and nothing made him lose his temper quicker than having her or anyone else disobey him. When he went into one of his spells of violent rage, during which he lost all control of himself and cursed and flailed anything or anybody within reach, it was sometimes two or three days before his anger ran its course. She hurried to her own room to comb her hair and change her clothes.

While she undressed she listened hopefully for some sound of Grady in the great house. Each time the creaking or the settling of an aging timber echoed through the building, she waited breathlessly with the hope that it was Grady coming down the hall to her room. In the silent loneliness of her room she could not keep from wondering over and over again where he had been and what he had been doing during the past three days and nights. She knew practically nothing about the persons he associated with when he was in Maguffin, the county seat fifteen miles away, but she did know he spent the greater part of the time away from home at a bar and gambling house operated by Skeeter Wilhite. She knew that much because Grady's first cousin, Ben Baxter, who practiced law in Maguffin, had told her several times during the winter that Grady was losing more money than he could afford, and that if he did not stay away from Skeeter Wilhite's, something disastrous was bound to happen. Grady frequently ran up a bill of sixty or seventy dollars in an evening at the bar when he treated the house to several rounds of drinks, and his gambling losses were sometimes in the hundreds of dollars. There were times when he finished the evening a winner at the dice table, but it was not unusual for him to bet his winnings on the turn of a red card and, nine times out of ten, with Skeeter himself shuffling the cards, he went away completely broke or heavily in debt.

Lucyanne had come to feel that it was useless to ask Grady each time he came home to tell her where he had been and what he had been doing, because each time she asked, he became more angry and abusive towards her. Even when he was in good spirits, which in itself was a rare occasion, he gave her a glib answer, vague and evasive, about being busy in town transacting important business. She knew the unconvincing story by heart now, after having listened to it so many times during the ten months they had been married. But she knew, just as Mama Elsie knew, that when Grady went away like that for days at a time, he nearly always had to mortgage more of the farm in order to pay his bar bills and gambling losses at Skeeter Wilhite's.

There was very little land left now. The Dunbar plantation originally had spread over more than five thousand acres of the richest and most productive land in that section of the country. For two generations the plantation had made money

at the rate of a hundred thousand dollars a year
from the rich upland cotton lands and virgin
stands of timber. Grady's father and grandfather
had never had to count the cost of anything their
hearts desired, but their good fortune had become Grady's misfortune. While inheriting their
spendthrift manner of living, he had also fallen
heir to depleted and eroded cotton fields and cut-
over timber lands. By the time he was twenty, the
plantation was losing money instead of making
it, and so, year by year, he had mortgaged a por-
tion of it in order to obtain spending money. Now,
after the numerous foreclosures, there was less
than two hundred acres of the original plantation
left.

The large three-story manor house with its rotting shingles and weather-warped clapboards,
which in the family's prime had been a magnificent structure and a renowned showplace, had
become dilapidated to such an extent that the
bank in Maguffin flatly refused to accept it as
security for a loan of even the most insignificant
amount. The house had suffered so severely from
neglect that the brick-and-mortar chimneys had
crumbled to roof-top level, which was the reason
no insurance company could be found to insure
the building against fire. The north wing had
sunk to the ground when the supporting brick

foundation crumbled, and when it rained, water seeped and trickled from walls and ceilings for days afterward. Whole sections of the roof had fallen, along with the rafters, to the now abandoned third floor. Each time Lucyanne had spoken to Grady about the condition of the house, he had become angry and dismissed the subject by telling her he had no money to waste on repairs and, besides, that it was good enough for her to live in the way it was.

At ten o'clock by her small silver-framed dressing-table clock, which was one of the presents her mother had given her when she was married, Grady still had not come to her room. Lucyanne opened the door to the hall and listened for several moments. There was no sound anywhere in the great house, and she went back and put on a dress she wanted Grady to see. Her mother had sent it to her and she had saved it to wear when Grady came home.

Tiptoeing noiselessly, she went into the dark silent hall. Mama Elsie was asleep, Martha had left for the night, and the great house was hushed and quiet. As she walked softly down the uncarpeted hall she could not keep from remembering, as though it were a bad dream, the many lonely nights she had spent waiting for Grady to come home, each time hoping and praying that when he did come back, he would come to her room. He was usually drunk and noisy, though, filling the house with his yells and curses until he fell drunkenly across his bed and slept until the following afternoon. At other times, like the present, he went quietly to his room and made no sound until morning.

When she reached Grady's door, she listened intently. There was no sound at all in his room. She shook back her hair, touching it quickly into place with her hands, and smoothed her dress into place. Then she reached for the knob. The door was locked. During all the time she was walking down the hall she had told herself over and over that the door would not be locked this time and that she would be able to go inside before Grady knew she was there. At any other time she would have cried with disappointment but now she was determined not to let herself break down and give up so easily. Trembling all over, she tapped softly on the wooden panel. There was an immediate stir inside the room, a slight creaking of the bed, and after that a deep silence. She waited as long as she could before saying anything, holding her breath until it was painful. The terrifying silence in the dark hall made her tremble with fear.

"Grady," she whispered in a quaking voice.

There was no response. The excited pounding of her heart throbbed through her body.

"It's me, Grady," she said beseechingly. "It's Lucyanne."

There was still no answer. Gripping her fingers tightly in the palms of her hands, she waited for him to speak to her.

"Please, Grady," she said when she could wait no longer, her voice rising in urgency and sounding tense in her ears. "I want to come in, Grady. Please let me."

Just as she finished speaking there was a quick movement somewhere in the room that sounded as though somebody had moved a chair. After that she tried again to turn the knob, but the lock was unyielding. She rattled the knob desperately.

"Please won't you let me come in with you, Grady?" she pleaded. "I want to so much! I haven't seen you in such a long time and I've missed you a lot, Grady."

After that she could hear his bare feet on the floor as he crossed the room. She knew he was standing on the other side of the door and her heart beat madly to know he was so close to her.

"Oh, Grady!" she cried.

"What do you want?" he said peevishly.

"I want you, Grady!" she told him, pounding the door with her hands. "I want to be with you,

Grady! That's all I want——just to be with you!"

"Not now," she heard him say. "Go on away."

"Please don't be so cruel, Grady! I can't stand it! If you'd only let me be with you for just a little while——"

"Go on back to your room."

"But, Grady, you've got to let me in!" she pleaded. "I've been so lonely——"

"I told you to go away, didn't I?" he said angrily.

She heard him walking away from the door and the knowledge that he was no longer there left her feeling helpless and distraught. In spite of all she could do to control herself, tears filled her eyes. Never before in her life had she felt as unwanted as she did then and it was an anguish she did not know how to endure. For three long days and nights she had waited for him to come back, telling herself over and over again that when he did come home this time, he would want her. Whenever doubts had filled her mind with scoffs and taunts, she had made herself believe that he had changed and that from that time on their life together would be different. What was happening now was tormenting and agonizing.

She could think of no single reason why Grady should not want to be with her. She was still attractive and youthful. Even Mama Elsie had grudgingly admitted that she was more than ordinarily beautiful and that she was in that way a distinct credit to the family. Ben Baxter had told her in his shy timid manner that she was the loveliest girl he had ever seen and that he had no desire to get married if he had to spend his life with someone who was second choice. She was dark-haired and slender with firmly rounded arms and legs and her skin was slightly tanned summer and winter. Her full generous mouth was quick to smile, and when she looked at a person, her soft brown eyes were intense and friendly. She knew Grady had once thought she was beautiful and desirable, because he had told her so many times before they were married. She had to have the feeling that she was wanted by somebody if she was going to continue living, otherwise she would rather be dead. Above everyone she knew, she wanted Grady to be the man who desired her, because she loved him and because he was her husband.

Frantically she beat on the door with her hands.

"Grady! Grady!" She was seized with sudden terror. The thought that someone else was in the room with him came to her for the first time. She had no idea who it could be, or how anyone could get into his room without her knowing about it, but what was more important right then than anything else was to find out whether or not her suspicions were true or false. "Grady! Grady!" she called again. "Let me in—let me in, Grady!"

"Get away from there, goddam it!" he shouted angrily from somewhere in the room. "I told you to go away and stop bothering me like this. I've had enough of it."

"I've got to come in, Grady," she said in a firm voice. "Open the door right away. I mean it, Grady. I won't stand for this."

"How many times do I have to tell you to go away, goddam it!" he shouted. "Stop pounding on that door and leave me alone!"

"You can't do this way, Grady," she said. "You can't—you can't! Let me in, Grady—let me in!"

"If you keep that up much longer, I'm coming out there and make you quit it. When I tell you to do something, I'm going to see to it that you do it."

Lucyanne stepped back from the door undecidedly. She was afraid of Grady, because she knew that when he lost his temper he was almost inhuman in his actions.

"There's somebody in there with you, Grady," she said determinedly. "I know there is. Who is it?"

She waited, trembling. By that time she was not sure that she wanted to know the truth, because if someone were with him, she knew she would have to leave, and she did not want to do that.

Grady remained silent. During the long period of time when nothing was said, she began to cry. She could not help herself. The tears, smarting and blinding, relieved the throbbing pain that had gripped her, and she leaned weakly against the wall.

"Are you still out there?" she heard Grady ask her.

"Yes, Grady," she said quickly, thinking he may have relented and was about to open the door.

"Well, go on away like I told you," he said gruffly.

She went down the hall towards her room. She had stopped crying by that time, but her sight was still blurred and she knew she might begin crying again any moment. After going into the room she glanced at herself in the mirror for an instant, quickly turning away from what she saw there. Her hair was untidy, her eyes were red and puffed, and the dress that she had wanted Grady to see, once so crisp and shapely, now hung bedraggledly from her shoulders. Opening the wide veranda doors, she left the room as quickly as she could and went to the railing.

She had been standing there in the cool darkness staring for a long time into the night when she heard the faint faraway sound of guitar music. Quickly sitting down, she looked out over the yard and saw the dim lamplight coming from the cabin doorways in the Negro quarter a hundred yards away. There were eight small one-room cabins in the quarter, each identical in size and appearance. They had been built of rough-hewn logs chinked with red clay, and had been put there by Grady's grandfather to house his slaves. They were now occupied by the Negro house servants and field hands. The cabins were as dilapidated and in want of repair as the great house of thirty-two rooms. There had never been windows in the cabins, because when they were built, it was the custom to lock the slaves in from sundown to sunrise, but there were small slits in the logs at each end of the building which ventilated the room to some extent and which were now covered with guano sacks. The pine-log stockade which had originally surrounded the group of cabins had been taken down, but otherwise the quarter had changed little in appearance in a hundred years.

The guitar music sounded closer and more distinct when Lucyanne leaned forward and rested her arms on the railing. The soft tones of the guitar floated all around her in the balmy night, filling her ears with a primitive sound. Presently she heard somebody singing in a plaintive voice. She had heard the song many times before but the words, when she had heard them, went unnoticed. Now the words sounded purposeful and meaningful. She sat up erectly as her whole body became tense.

> *Good gal went and lost her man,*
> *Bad gal up and took him away....*

A piercing painful shiver stabbed at her. The mockery of the song was unbearable.

She jumped to her feet and ran across the veranda. Just as she reached the door, however, she hesitated. She wanted to go back and make Grady let her into his room so she could see with her own eyes whether or not she had justly suspected him. As she stood undecidedly at the door, she slowly realized that going back would be useless. He would never let her into his room now, even if he were alone, because she had made him angry. She knew by past experiences that he was going to make her suffer for days. His face would be flushed with sullen anger and he would defiantly refuse to speak to her until his resentment had run its course. He had always been like that, and as he grew older the streaks of moroseness became longer in duration. He was almost habitually sullen now. Like Mama Elsie, he had grown to find pleasure in being curt and short-tempered and derived satisfaction from his power to hurt others.

Lucyanne went back to the railing and stood in the darkness of the veranda looking out across the white sandy yard. Over the fields half a mile away she could see a single twinkling light shining from the overseer's house. That was where Will Harrison lived. Farther away, on the other side of the river, there were numerous pale starlike lights shining in the clear night. There was the appearance of happiness and contentment all around her, in farm house, tenant house, and cabin alike. What she saw daunted her and made her more miserable than ever.

Music swept over the yard from the quarter.

> *Oh, Lordy, I'm gettin' blue,*
> *Oh, Lordy, what'll I do. . . .*

She sat down abruptly, listening to the compelling sounds. The words made her think all over again of all the long nights she had waited for Grady, trying to be patient and understanding but wondering why he avoided her. Almost every night she had waited for him to come to her and, when he failed to come, she had gone to his room. Sometimes he had locked his door, as he had done this time; other times when he was not in his room, she had waited nevertheless. Many nights she had lain on his bed until dawn, sleepless, and when he still did not come back, she went to her own room and cried herself to sleep. When she married Grady, she had not imagined anything like this would happen to her, and now after almost a year she could not understand the strange perverse streak in Grady's nature that made him treat her this way. The more she thought about it, the less confident she became in her own security. For all she knew, she could walk out of the house and Grady would never go a step to bring her back. She had even come to believe that that was what both he and Mama Elsie wanted her to do. She knew that if she were not in love with Grady, and deeply so, she would have walked out of his life months before.

That, however, was only one of many things she did not understand. She could not understand being told that he had never intended to practice law, even though he had graduated from law school and had passed the state bar examinations a month before they were married. When she had asked Mama Elsie why Grady refused to practice the profession he had fitted himself for, she was told in Mama Elsie's superior manner that no

Dunbar had to engage in business or to practice a profession for a livelihood, and that education, for a Dunbar, was solely a matter of culture and pride. After that Lucyanne had tried to prod Grady into doing something by pointing out how useless his existence would be if he allowed Mama Elsie's philosophy to ruin his life. Grady was not concerned. She had finally given up when she saw how impossible it was for her to break through his shell of indifference.

A girl's voice, pitched to a high note, swept over the yard with a plaintive cry.

> *If he'll give me one more try,*
> *I'll give him lovin' till I die. . . .*

The music, carrying the words of the song in a swelling tide of rhythm, was disturbing and upsetting. There seemed to be no end to it. Every night it was the same. Sitting in their chairs in front of the cabins, the Negroes played the guitar and sang until midnight or later, but long after they had gone to bed, Lucyanne could hear the haunting music ringing in her ears.

She covered her face with her hands.

"Please stop," she sobbed. "I can't stand it any longer! Please stop!"

> *I'm just a poor gal strugglin' along,*
> *But I got my man, I got my man. . . .*

Chapter IV

Grady slept all morning behind the locked door, not even getting up when Martha brought his lunch on a tray and begged him at least to drink some hot coffee. The tray, covered with a white napkin, was still untouched outside his door when Ben Baxter drove up and stopped his car in front of the house at four o'clock that afternoon. It had been a hot cloudless day, but in midafternoon a breeze began blowing from the coast, and Lucyanne had gone to the downstairs veranda to sit in the cool air. A Negro field hand was plowing with a team of mules on the slope below the house and two tractors, droning monotonously all day long, were disking the cotton field on the ridge above. Undisturbed by the noise of the tractor engines, Mama Elsie was in the north wing taking her usual afternoon nap.

Ben got out of the car and waved his hand energetically at Lucyanne. She had felt a quickening of her pulse the moment she recognized who he was, and now she felt a rising excitement in her breast as she watched his lanky figure when he came up the brick wall to the veranda. Ben was in his thirties, about the same age as Grady, and several years older than Lucyanne. Although he was unmistakably a Dunbar in appearance, which was only natural since his mother and Grady's father had been brother and sister, he was unlike the others in character. In fact, he was so much unlike a Dunbar that he had often been called the black sheep of the family. He was considerate, soft-spoken, and completely unselfish. Lucyanne had liked Ben the first time she met him, and she always felt much more at ease with him than she had ever felt with Grady.

She stood up when he reached the steps, an eager smile spreading over her face. Ben stopped and looked at her intently for several moments before running up the steps to the veranda. She held out her hand and he gripped it in both of his for a long time before either said anything. A sudden persistent thought raced through her mind while she looked up into his face. She wondered which of the two, Grady or Ben, she would have married if she had met them both at the same time.

"How are you, Lucyanne?" Ben asked in his quiet way. "You look wonderful."

"Oh, Ben, it's awfully good to see you again!" she said quickly, lowering her gaze so he would not see the look in her eyes.

"I hope it's all right for me to drop in like this," he said uneasily.

"Of course it is, Ben," she assured him, glancing briefly at him. "You know that, Ben."

He finally released her hand and sat down on the railing. She sat down in the chair before him and watched him take out a pack of cigarettes. He offered her one, but she shook her head. He smoked in silence for several moments.

There had been a time when everybody in the county said with a shaking of the head that Ben Baxter was going to turn out to be another Grady Dunbar. In those days he had lived just as recklessly and heedlessly as Grady had ever done, spending his inheritance in a continuous wild splurge with no regard for his responsibilities. During his mother's lifetime she allowed him to indulge in every whim, regardless of cost, and after her death he spent what money remained in a few months. Then one morning he woke up in a Boston hotel room broke, hungry, and without a friend who would help him. He was then within a year of finishing his education at Harvard. Instead of coming home and living on his relatives, as everyone in Maguffin expected him to do, he got a part-time job and worked his way through his last year at college. He did not even come home to spend his summer vacation, but instead stayed in Boston and worked. He was not seen in Maguffin for three years, but at the end of that time he came back with a degree in law and took a job at twenty dollars a week as a clerk in a lawyer's office. Ben was a law clerk for two years, during which time few persons in Maguffin believed that the change would be permanent. Nearly everyone in town confidently expected him to revert at any moment to the ways of the Dunbars and Baxters. Instead, he resigned from his job and opened his own law office. His first caller was Judge Lovejoy, the county political leader, who had become so impressed by Ben's strong-willed determination that he offered Ben the prospect of a well-rewarded future in politics in exchange for Ben's loyalty. He had promptly declined Judge Lovejoy's offer, saying that he preferred to keep his independence. The decision was costly. Judge Lovejoy left his office in stormy temper, and after that clients were few. After a time, though, it became generally known among indigent whites and chattel-mortgaged Negroes that the most helpful and least expensive legal advice in the county could always be obtained from Ben Baxter.

He got up from the railing and sat down in the chair beside Lucyanne.

"You haven't been in town recently," he said. "You are becoming a homebody, Lucyanne."

"That's what I'm beginning to think, Ben. But I just haven't wanted to go anywhere."

"That's not good for you, Lucyanne. You shouldn't let yourself stay out here all alone all the time, not seeing anybody week after week."

"There's Grady," she said quickly. "And Mama Elsie."

Ben nodded gravely. She could see him watching her thoughtfully and she wondered what he was really thinking deep down inside of him. She turned her head to keep him from seeing the unhappiness that her eyes would not conceal. Seeing her turn her face away, Ben looked out across the yard and down the slope at the bottom land along the river.

"Grady's in Maguffin more than he's at home," he reminded her. "And when he is here—he's not really here, is he, Lucyanne?"

She knew instantly what Ben meant. What he had said was a statement of fact, and not a question she was expected to answer. She turned towards him, trying to smile bravely, but the gesture was useless, because after that she realized it was useless to try to hide her feelings from Ben any longer.

"I guess you know what's happening between us, Ben," she said with a sigh. "There's not much sense in my trying to hide it."

"I know you're miserably unhappy, Lucyanne," he said with concern.

She looked down at her hands in her lap.

"Did Grady come home last night?" Ben asked her.

She nodded.

"Where is he now?"

"I don't know."

"Is he upstairs in his room?"

"I suppose so."

"Have you talked to him since he came back this time—did he say anything at all?"

"What do you mean, Ben?"

"Has he told you about his troubles—his latest troubles?"

She shook her head. "I don't know anything about Grady's affairs, Ben. He rarely ever tells me anything at all about what he's doing."

"I thought that was the way it was," he said gravely.

Ben propped his feet on the railing and sat staring thoughtfully at the pine-covered hills on the other side of the river. Lucyanne waited, wondering why he had asked those particular questions. She knew he was seriously concerned about something.

"Lucyanne," he said, still not looking at her.

"What is it, Ben?" she asked tensely.

He put his feet on the floor and leaned forward, resting his elbows on his knees. He still did not look directly at her.

"I'm afraid there's going to be a certain amount of—of unpleasantness," he began, "and I think you ought to know about it. That's why I came out here this afternoon. I wanted to be sure that you knew what was happening."

"What are you talking about, Ben?"

"There's going to be some trouble, Lucyanne."

"What kind of trouble?" she asked fearfully. "What are you talking about?"

"Just to make everything more disagreeable, there are two batches of trouble this time instead of the usual one."

"He's been gambling again and lost a lot of money, hasn't he?"

"Twenty-five hundred this time, Lucyanne. That's a lot of money. Grady can't raise that much any more."

"Maybe he can borrow it at the bank," she said hopefully.

"No. The bank wouldn't lend it, to Grady. No private lender would either."

"What will he do, Ben? What can he do?"

"I don't know. I'd lend it to him if I had it, Lucyanne, for your sake, but I don't have that kind of money. I'm afraid this is one time I can't help him. What's left of this farm is already mortgaged to the hilt, there are liens on the tractors, and that pair of mules Grady owns wouldn't bring a hundred dollars at auction, even if they weren't already mortgaged. There's not a man in the county who would sign Grady's note in his right mind. That's the way things are. The Dunbars are just about finished, Lucyanne."

"You mean it's really that hopeless, Ben?"

He nodded.

"Poor Grady," she said sadly. "I feel awfully sorry for him sometimes. I really do, in spite of everything. I just can't help it. Maybe it's because he's my husband, maybe it's just my nature. But every time he gets into trouble I feel the same way. A lot of times I think it really isn't his fault that these awful things happen to him. He can't help being what he is. It's the curse of growing up in this family more than anything else. Being born a Dunbar is what has ruined him. If he'd only go away somewhere and get away from this rotting evil house, he'd have a better chance. As long as he stays in this unhealthy atmosphere he's going to keep on thinking that the world owes him a living just because he's a Dunbar. I'd stick by him, no matter how poor we were, if he'd only go away, far away, and work for a living. He could do it if he wanted to. But no," she added bitterly, "Mama Elsie would consider that beneath the dignity of a Dunbar."

"Have you ever talked to Grady about going away?"

"Grady won't listen to me, Ben. I've tried every way I know how to get him to talk about it, but if I keep on, he loses his temper and gets into a rage that lasts for days and days. When that happens, he often won't speak to me for a week at a time. Rather than have to endure that, I try not to antagonize him. I know I should try, and keep on trying, but it seems so hopeless."

There was a loud commotion in the house. Presently they could hear Grady's heavy footsteps as he came down the stairway. Ben and Lucyanne glanced at each other apprehensively. Ben stood up.

Chapter V

BARELY TAKING NOTICE OF either of them, Grady strode heavily around the veranda to the south side of the house. Almost as soon as he was out of sight they heard him shout gruffly. Wondering what was taking place at the side entrance, Ben and Lucyanne hurried to the corner.

When they got there, they saw Grady standing at the top of the steps and Uncle Jeff Davis Jackson, one of the Negroes who lived in the quarter, waiting in the yard. Uncle Jeff Davis was the oldest Negro on the place, both he and his wife, Aunt Bessie, having been born in the quarter and named by Grady's grandfather. They had one son, Sammy, who was raised in the quarter and who had been away in the army for two years. Sammy was back now but, instead of coming back to work for Grady, he had a job at the saw mill in Maguffin.

Ben and Lucyanne could see Grady glaring down angrily at Uncle Jeff Davis, who stood humbly in the yard with hat in hand. The old white-haired Negro nervously shuffled his sprawling broken shoes on the hard sandy yard.

"What do you want to see me about?" Grady asked him roughly. "What do you mean by sending Martha to tell me you want to see me at this time of day?"

"Please, sir, Mr. Grady, I hate to bother you like this," Uncle Jeff Davis began in a trembling voice, "but I want to ask a little favor of you and I was scared you might be going off again before I had a chance to speak to you, please, sir." In his anxiety not to displease Grady any more than necessary, he began stumbling nervously over his words.

"Well, go ahead and say it and stop that mumbling," Grady said irritatedly. "But next time wait until you see me come out of the house. I don't like having niggers send for me."

Shuffling his feet on the sand, Uncle Jeff Davis bowed and mumbled apologetically.

"Please, sir, Mr. Grady, all the little I want is for you to let me and my wife move off to town. We're getting old, both of us, and I ain't fit to work all day out in the fields like I used to could. The heat just acts like the old devil himself out to get me every time I go out and try to do a day's work. If it wasn't for that, I wouldn't want to quit and move away to Maguffin. And if I wasn't getting so old I wouldn't mind the heat or nothing else because I sure do thank you for letting me work for you all this time, Mr. Grady, but me and my wife ain't got much longer to live, noway, and we only want a little rest before the time comes to go. Please, sir, Mr. Grady, can we do that?"

"Hell, no!" Grady shouted angrily. "What makes you think you can leave here and go off to live some place else? Who's fed you all your life and given you a house to live in?"

"You has, Mr. Grady. Both you and your daddy before you done that. I sure do thank you for what you and him both done for me and my folks."

"Then what makes you think you can haul off and leave here without paying me for all that?"

"Pay you, Mr. Grady?" Uncle Jeff Davis said in a startled voice.

"You heard me! You're not deaf!"

"Seems like to me, Mr. Grady, I done gone and worked it all out in all these years. I don't know how many years it's been, but it's been a heap of them, 'way back ever since I was old enough to stand up and walk between the plow handles. Seems like that ought to be long enough to work out the pay for the house and vittles."

"Who put this idea in your head about leaving? Who've you been talking to?"

"My boy, Sammy, please, sir. He came back from the war not long ago and got himself a good-paying job at the saw mill in Maguffin that pays him real money every Saturday night and he say he wants me and his mother to come to town and live with him, because he makes enough wages to rent a house for all of us to stay together."

"I've been wondering where he was," Grady said. "Why didn't he come back here and go to work for me instead of getting a job in town? Doesn't he know better than that?"

Uncle Jeff Davis began to shake spasmodically as though he had chills-and-fever. He twisted his frayed field-straw hat in his trembling hands and looked down at the ground.

"You heard what I asked you! Why didn't he come back here and go to work where he be-longs?"

"I reckon it's because you don't pay out real wages in money, Mr. Grady," he said fearfully. "Sammy'd rather work for real money at the saw mill, than only get some old clothes or something once in a while."

"He's turned out to be one of these goddam uppity niggers," Grady said. "He'd better stay in town, because if I ever catch him around here, I'll knock some sense into him. I don't want to hear niggers talk like that. You understand what I said, Uncle Jeff Davis?"

"Yes, sir, Mr. Grady. I know what you said."

"All right, then. Get back on to the quarter where you belong and don't ever let me hear any more of that biggity talk out of you again."

Uncle Jeff Davis shuffled his feet on the sandy yard, his hands picking nervously at the frayed edges of his hat. He moved backward a few steps, but he did not leave. Grady watched him surlily.

"Goddam it, what are you standing there for like that?" Grady shouted. "You heard what I said. Why don't you do what I told you? Get on back to the quarter!"

"Please, sir, Mr. Grady," he said beseechingly, "I ain't aiming not to do exactly like you said, but I sure do want to move to town. Please, sir, me and my wife want to do that mighty much, Mr. Grady. I know you ain't the kind who'd give out hard dealings to the colored, because your daddy used to——"

"Shut up!" he said. "I've heard enough out of you!" He moved down the steps to the yard in a threatening manner. "You're going to stay here.

How many times do I have to tell you that?"

"But, Mr. Grady, ain't there some way of letting me and my wife off?"

"Sure," Grady said with a short laugh. "All you have to do is pay me what you owe me for keep."

"How much would that come to, Mr. Grady?" Uncle Jeff Davis asked hopefully.

"Five hundred dollars."

The old Negro's head moved slowly from side to side. Drops of tears glistened on his cheeks. His shoulders slumped downward and downward.

"Five hundred dollars," he said partly aloud, still shaking his head dispiritedly. "Mr. Grady, you know good and well I ain't got nothing like that and never had. I ain't had that much money in all the years I worked for you and your daddy both. Your daddy didn't believe in paying out real money for wages, neither, and all I ever got from him was some old clothes and a sack of cow peas now and then, like you give me sometimes. That's why I ain't able to pay you what you say I owe. But I sure enough would give it to you if I had it."

"Then get on away from here and stop arguing about it," Grady ordered. "I'm tired of listening to you. And after this I don't want to hear any more complaining out of you, either."

"But, please, sir, looks like you ought to do a little favor like that for me, after all these years when I ain't never asked for nothing much but a little something to eat now and then. I'm too old just like I said to do much good no more on the land. I just naturally ain't fit for hard work no more. My time's pretty near up, anyhow."

"I'll tell you when to quit work, and I don't want to hear of you quitting and running away, either. I know how to handle runaway niggers. I'll have the sheriff's bloodhounds after you so quick you'll think lightning struck you."

"Then, please, sir, Mr. Grady, maybe you'll just let my wife move to town, because she's got the rheumatism something awful in her back and it pains her to stoop over the washtubs like she has to do. If you won't let both us go, please, sir, just let her go. I'd be mighty thankful to you for all the rest of my life, Mr. Grady."

Grady picked up a broken axe handle that was standing on end against the steps. He swung the handle back and forth in front of him several times, forcing Uncle Jeff Davis to back away from him.

"Go on back to the quarter and keep your nigger mouth shut from now on," he said. He moved towards the Negro, swinging the axe handle in a wide arc. "If you ever come up here again with that kind of biggity talk, it'll be the last time. I've heard all from you that I'm going to stand for."

Uncle Jeff Davis backed away, keeping beyond Grady's reach. When he got to the edge of the yard, where the path to the quarter began, he turned around and hurried towards the cabins, glancing back over his shoulder from time to time until he was out of sight.

Still swinging the heavy stick, Grady turned and walked across the yard to the corner of the house where Ben and Lucyanne were standing at the veranda railing.

"Well, what do you want?" he said to Ben. "What did you come out here for, to hand out some free advice?"

"Listen, Grady," Ben said earnestly, leaning over the railing and looking down at his cousin, "why don't you do the big thing and let that old Negro go where he wants to? He's too old to work any more. You know that. You're only making him stay here because you're angry at Sammy Jackson for not coming back out here to work for you. That's not right. The only decent thing to do is to let Uncle Jeff Davis leave. You know that, Grady."

"No nigger's going to come to me and tell me what he's going to do."

"Let's forget that for a minute, Grady," Ben said. "The important thing is to be considerate of any human being, white or black. That old Negro has as much right to live his life the way he wants to as you have. You seem to have forgotten that, if you ever realized it. He doesn't owe you a red cent—you owe him money. Now, why don't you call the whole thing square and let him go? That's the only decent thing to do, Grady."

Grady slung the axe handle across the yard with all his might. His face flushed with anger.

"I know how to treat niggers to make them stay in their place, and I'm going to keep on doing it, too. It's nigger-lovers like you who stir up all the trouble, going around saying niggers are as good as white people. Where would this country be if we listened to your kind of talk? I can tell you! The niggers would run wild, that's what! They'd rape every white woman in the country, and shoot every white man. Go on up North if that's the way you're going to talk, because we don't want you down here. We're going to keep the niggers in their place, whether you and your kind like it or not."

"You're not using your head, Grady," Ben said. "Times have changed. Everybody in this country has certain fundamental rights. Take Uncle Jeff Davis for example——"

"I've heard enough of that," Grady said with a sweep of his hand. He turned abruptly and started walking towards the rear of the house. "If you nigger-lovers had your way, you'd undo all the good that's been done in the past hundred years."

After he had gone, Ben nodded to Lucyanne and she followed him across the veranda and down the front steps. They walked silently to Ben's car in the driveway.

"That was the other thing I was going to tell you about, Lucyanne," he said. "That's the other batch of trouble."

"What do you mean, Ben?"

"Sammy Jackson came to my office several days ago and told me he wanted to move his parents to town. He knew as well as I did that Grady was going to say they couldn't leave, and he asked me to advise him what to do. I arranged with Sammy to have his father come up here this afternoon and ask Grady for permission to leave, and that's how I came to be here at the time. I wanted to be present and hear what was said, because I thought I might be able to persuade Grady to let Uncle Jeff Davis and his wife go. You saw how unsuccessful I was."

"But maybe you can still talk Grady into letting them leave," she suggested.

"I don't think so. It's probably going to take

legal action to change Grady's mind. As long as he can keep them here, by means of threats or otherwise, he gets their labor for practically nothing. He's got the system working like a charm. His father did the same thing. Grady can keep a Negro family in perpetual debt by charging more on the account books for food and housing than he credits them for labor, and at any time when it looks as if they might work themselves out of debt, he can put them right back again merely by charging them on the books for some imaginary medical supplies or the like. Of course, if they could read, they could demand to see the books and protest, but when did Grady ever let a Negro child go to school to learn to read?"

"Is it really that bad, Ben?"

"Or worse," he nodded. "What it amounts to is that no Negro on the place can ever get out of debt to Grady. But times change faster than a Dunbar, and I've decided to boost them along a little."

"What are you going to do?"

"I'm going to give Grady one last fair chance to let Uncle Jeff Davis and Aunt Bessie leave, as well as any of the other Negroes living on the place, and if he refuses, which he will, I'm going to take it upon myself to see that the law steps in and breaks up this little private domain of peonage. Grady isn't the only one in the county who's doing it. I know of at least half a dozen other landowners who need to be jolted out of the practice. I won't get any help from Judge Lovejoy, because it wouldn't be good politics, and they may even try to keep me quiet, but I'm going to open up the case if it ruins me. There's no place for such things in this country any longer."

"But even if you do give Grady another chance, you know he's not going to let them leave. Grady's too hard-headed to do that, Ben."

"Then I'll go ahead and buck Grady," he said with determination. "Kinship will have to go by the board, if that's the case. I'll do anything else I can for Grady, because we've always been good friends, and I like him, and we're first cousins. I'll do my best to help him raise that money he needs, or try to get the debt settled some way. But, just the same, I'm going through with this other thing."

He opened the door of his car and sat down under the steering wheel. Lucyanne, still silent, saw him start the engine.

"Well," Ben said, smiling uneasily, "I hope you don't hate me for this, Lucyanne. But it's the way I feel, and I've got to do it. I wanted you to know why."

"I don't hate you for it, Ben," she told him,

going to the door of the car and putting her hand on his arm. "I admire you for it. I didn't know anything like that was going on. I thought the Negroes could leave any time they wished to. Nobody ever told me they had to stay here. I had no idea it was anything like that."

"There're probably a lot of other people who didn't know about it," he said. "We'll see if we can enlighten them—and Grady, too."

Chapter VI

GRADY HAD HIS DINNER served in his room that evening, and Lucyanne sat through another long silent meal in the reproachful presence of Mama Elsie. The contrived subtlety of the older woman's silence was agonizing and tormenting. When the ordeal was over at last, Lucyanne ran upstairs to her room.

Once more she put on the new dress she wanted Grady to see, and carefully brushed her hair. Then, filled with hope, she ran down the hall. This time Grady's door was not locked and it swung open easily when she turned the knob. She found herself standing breathlessly in the middle of the room.

He was not there. As she stood gazing at the rumpled empty bed and the large chair with the shaded reading lamp beside it, she felt the familiar pain of misery strike at her. She went to the bed and sat down dejectedly, trying to make herself believe that he would come back. After half an hour she got up and walked down the dark stairway and left the house.

A full yellowish moon had come up over the river, and for a long time she wandered aimlessly in the night, walking through the lacy pattern of shadows on the white sandy yard. The nightbirds, fluttering among the branches of the oaks, chirped and chattered incessantly, and somewhere out in the fields a raincrow, perched in a persimmon tree, cried mournfully.

Through the anguish of her mind she became aware of soft laughter and guitar music. The overwhelming beat of the rhythm made her heart race excitedly. Night after night, when she allowed herself to listen, she had heard the same primitive tune and the song with its seemingly endless number of verses.

Now when night falls on the land,
They all can hear the poor gal plead. . . .

Lucyanne ran across the yard to the front of the house. Grady's car was still standing where he had left it the night before under the portico and she was certain he had not gone back to town. She knew then that the quarter was the only place he could be. She had never been down there after dark, and Grady had often told her to stay away from there at all times, but now she knew she had to go.

Leaving the portico, she walked firmly across the front yard, around the house, and to the path that led down to the quarter. Another Negro girl had taken up the song and was singing in a wild abandoned voice. Lucyanne stopped and listened to her.

> *Sweet man, I've had it tough,*
> *Sweet man, come strut your stuff;*
> *Makes no mind what you wish,*
> *I'll always be your heapin' dish. . . .*

Lucyanne began walking resolutely down the path between the rows of blossoming peach trees. At first she could hear waves of slow lazy laughter, throaty and carefree, but when she approached the first cabin, the laughter suddenly vanished completely.

A baby began to cry, and she heard a woman's urgent voice say, "Hush, you child, hush!" As she walked on, she could see small groups of Negroes sitting in chairs in the front yards of the cabins. One by one, the groups became silent and motionless as she was seen and recognized.

Lucyanne walked past the first two cabins, and when she was in front of the third, she saw one of the women get up from a rocking chair in the yard and come towards her. She stopped when she recognized Martha, who waddled laboriously to the path. The other Negroes, she could tell in a glance, were watching her apprehensively.

"Is that you, Miss Lucyanne?" Martha whispered with rising inflection of her husky voice. Martha looked even larger and more fleshy than ever in the yellow moonlight. As usual, summer and winter alike, she was barefooted. "It is you, ain't it, Miss Lucyanne?"

Lucyanne made no reply, because she knew that Martha had recognized her in the beginning.

"My goodness me, Miss Lucyanne, what is you doing out so late in the night like this, all by yourself? You want me to go up to the big house and do something or other for you, Miss Lucyanne, mam?"

"No, Martha," she replied quickly. "There's nothing to be done up there now."

Martha peered at her intently in the bright moonlight. She was curious and uncertain.

"It's going on eleven o'clock, or more, Miss Lucyanne. I'd done been in bed myself by this time iffen it hadn't turned sort of warm and stuffy, but I wanted to get me a little of the fresh air that's stirring around tonight. Iffen you ain't used to the night air, you might go and catch something real bad being out like this. There's a heap of plaguing things you can't always see in the dark."

"I'm looking for Mr. Grady," Lucyanne spoke up impatiently. "Have you seen him, Martha?"

"No, mam!" she replied at once with a startling promptness.

"Martha!" Lucyanne spoke curtly.

Martha's huge round head sank slowly into the round fold of flesh on her shoulders as she made an obvious pretense of reconsidering the question. Finally, she looked up at Lucyanne with a pained innocent expression.

"You mean has I seen Mr. Grady lately, Miss Lucyanne?" she asked.

"You know exactly what I mean, Martha."

"Does I, Miss Lucyanne?"

"Yes, you do!"

"Well," she began hesitantly, "maybe iffen I stopped and went to thinking back a little——"

"Have you seen Mr. Grady at all?" Lucyanne asked her pointedly.

Martha picked at the hem of her apron thoughtfully.

"Come to think of it, I recall seeing Mr. Grady just a little while before dark when he came back from town," the Negro woman replied in a manner of complete innocence. "Now that you freshen my mind, I'm sure dead positive about that, because that's when I had Mr. Grady's supper all ready for him, but he didn't eat it at all, and that's when I asked you iffen you wanted me to keep his supper warm for him on the cookstove. I'm truthfully positive about that now, Miss Lucyanne."

"That was last night, Martha, and you know it!"

"Was it? Well, I declare! Time sure does have a way of slipping by, don't it, Miss Lucyanne?"

"Never mind that, Martha. Have you seen Mr. Grady tonight—since dark?"

Martha was nervous and uncomfortable. She turned and glanced behind her at the group of silent Negroes sitting stiff and erect in the yard. After that she looked at Lucyanne again, but quickly averting her eyes and looking down at the path where her toes were methodically smoothing the sand. One of the babies began crying, and a woman in the yard got up hurriedly and went into the cabin.

"Why don't you answer me, Martha?" Lucyanne asked crossly. "You heard what I asked you, and you know exactly what I want to know. What makes you behave like this? All I want to know is if you've seen Mr. Grady tonight. Now, go ahead and tell me!"

Martha swallowed hard, the whites of her eyes swimming to and fro in the black pool of her face as she tried to keep from looking directly at Lucyanne.

"Miss Lucyanne, I sure does wish you'd go on back up there to the big house," she said with an urgent earnestness. "Please go on back up there, Miss Lucyanne, like I want you to do."

"Why?" Lucyanne asked her, laughing nervously. "Why do you say such a thing, Martha?"

"Because I just naturally feel it deep down in my bones that it ain't going to do nobody no good iffen you don't, that's why, Miss Lucyanne. Please, mam, go on back up there like I say."

"But I'm looking for Mr. Grady, Martha. That's the reason I came down here. I've looked everywhere else. Why shouldn't I look in the quarter, too?"

"Because that's why I want you to go on back, Miss Lucyanne. This here ain't no place for you to be looking for him. Now, please, mam, do like I say."

"You're being very silly, Martha," she said with increasing irritation. "What's come over you? I've never heard you talk like this before."

"I sure do hope and pray I never have to do it again, neither," she said, her words becoming indistinct and mumbly, and her mountainous breasts heaving with agitation.

"Well, at least you can tell me this time if you've seen Mr. Grady tonight, Martha," Lucyanne told her sharply.

Tears began flowing down Martha's cheeks and she made no effort to wipe them away with her apron. She just stood sobbing and looking sorrowfully at Lucyanne. When she could stand it no longer, Lucyanne reached out and shook Martha's arm roughly.

"It don't make no difference iffen I saw Mr. Grady or iffen I didn't, Miss Lucyanne, because I just naturally know either way it's going to make trouble, that real bad old troublesome trouble, and I sure don't want to see none of that at all. Iffen you'd only just pay me some mind and do like I say——"

"Stop that kind of talk instantly, Martha! I don't want to hear another word of it!"

"Yessum," she muttered, subdued.

"Now, tell me the truth," Lucyanne said firmly. "Have you seen Mr. Grady tonight?"

"Yessum," she replied reluctantly.

"And you're sure you're telling me the truth?"
"Yessum."

"When was the last time you saw him?"
"Just a little while ago."

"Did he come down this way?"

"Yessum."

"And he's still down here?"

"Yessum."

"Where is he now?"

A renewed flow of tears bathed her huge cheeks, making her face glisten and sparkle in the moonlight. Her enormous breasts shook and heaved with unrestrained sobs. Before she realized what she was doing, Lucyanne was crying, too, but she quickly wiped the tears from her eyes and tried to keep Martha from noticing it.

"You haven't answered my question, Martha," she said, speaking rapidly in order to keep her voice under control. "You know what I want to know."

"Miss Lucyanne, please don't make me say that," she begged. "I'd rather have to go and do most anything else in the world."

Lucyanne was certain by that time that Grady was somewhere in the quarter. She had tried to keep the thought from her mind, but the suspicion had become stronger than her will to ignore it. It was the same painful distrust that had kept her awake night after night.

"You're certain Mr. Grady is down here in the quarter, Martha?" she asked the Negress.

"Yessum."

She gasped for breath before she could speak again.

"Then show me where he is."

"I'll have to show you iffen you make me do it, Miss Lucyanne," she said tearfully, "but I wouldn't iffen you didn't, because I just naturally know it's going to make trouble—mean, bad, ugly old trouble. I just know Mr. Grady'd tear the hide off me iffen he found out I went and told about him. All my life I've tried to stay out of white folks' way, and it looks like the devil is out to get me in trouble for dodging him all this time. I told that fool gal to quit messing around, because I knew she'd get caught up with one of these times, but she wouldn't mind narry a word I said."

"Never mind that now, Martha. Show me where he is."

"Yessum," Martha said resignedly. She sighed deeply. "Yessum," she repeated, shaking her head to herself, and began walking down the path. "It's down this way a piece."

Chapter VII

LUCYANNE FOLLOWED MARtha past two more of the cabins, the silent staring gaze of the Negroes in their chairs following her mercilessly. She could hear, as though far away, the muted dismal sound of guitar strings being fingered speculatively by one of the Negroes. All at once she wanted to turn and run home as fast as she could, but she knew she could never leave now. She followed Martha's sprawling waddling shape and tried to keep from thinking too much about where she was and what she was there for.

Martha stopped in the path in front of the next to the last cabin in the quarter. The cabin door, unlike the others, was closed, but dim lamplight was shining ominously through the crack over the threshold. The soft subdued tones of the guitar had become persistent and tantalizing.

Twitching nervously, Martha shifted the weight

of her body from one foot to the other, at the same time emitting from the depths of her body sorrowful moans. Tiny beads of perspiration, silver in the moonlight, appeared on her forehead. Lucyanne grasped her hands together to keep from trembling so much.

"Who lives here, Martha?" she asked in a quaking whisper that was almost inaudible.

"Sallie John," she replied bitterly.

Sallie John was an eighteen-year-old quadroon with delicately tinted skin and naturally straight black hair. She had been a maid in the house for two years. Shortly after Lucyanne married Grady and came there to live, Martha had intimated in her usual roundabout manner that it would be wise to put another and less personable girl in her place and to send Sallie John out to work with the field hands. Lucyanne had paid little attention to the remark at the time, soon forgetting that Martha had ever warned her against Sallie John. During the past several months, though, Lucyanne had grown to be suspicious of Sallie John. The girl, she had discovered at last, went out of her way to be bold and enticing in Grady's presence. On numerous occasions when she was serving dinner, she had leaned over Grady more than necessary, casually touching his arm or shoulder. And once when she took Grady's dinner to his room, Lucyanne had looked through the partly open door and seen Sallie John sitting on his bed. She went in immediately and sent the girl away.

"Are you sure he's in there, Martha?" she managed to ask in spite of the tenseness that gripped her throat.

"Yessum," Martha said nervously, "but please listen to me, Miss Lucyanne, and don't go in there." Tears began to flow easily down her gleaming black cheeks as she undertook to make a final desperate plea. Her large round lips quivered. "Please come on away from here and let me take you back to the big house, Miss Lucyanne. Can't nothing but trouble come now iffen you stay around here and don't do like I say. I'm an old woman, Miss Lucyanne, and I know what I'm saying. I've seen a heap of trouble-making things in my time, and I know good and well what I'm talking about when I say this here is the worst. Iffen you'll go on back to the big house, I promise to take that gal by the nape of her neck and shake some sense into her head the first thing in the morning. Now, iffen you'll only pay me some mind and do like I say——"

"No, Martha," she said with determination. "I know what I'm doing. I'm not going back to the house now. I'm going in that cabin."

"But you don't know that Sallie John like I do, Miss Lucyanne. She's a regular she-devil when it comes to getting what she's after. When that fool gal sets her mind on something, can't nothing stop her. I know what I'm talking about. Iffen she makes up her mind not to let you go in there and take Mr. Grady away, she's liable to do you some harm. I told her to quit messing around, but she wouldn't pay me no mind at all. Just because her skin ain't black, she thinks there ain't nothing in this big world she can't do. I told her she was a black nigger inside, just like me, and to watch her step around white folks, but she just laughed at me and said she could get anything in the world she takes a liking to, from the whites or the blacks. I never did like to hear a colored person talk like that, because sooner or later trouble is bound to come. I could tell you a heap about that Sallie John, because she's always hanging around the kitchen and bragging about her way with white folks, specially with Mr. Grady, and sometimes with other white men. I ain't never heard such boasting, so high and mighty. The other day me and her was tidying up Mr. Grady's room and the first thing I knew, that gal had plopped herself on Mr. Grady's bed and was bouncing around and cutting up like she belonged there. She started telling me what a good man he could be with her.

and I tell you I got myself out of there as fast as my feet'd travel, because I——"

"I don't want to hear any more, Martha! If you can't keep from talking like that, I don't want you around me! Do you understand?"

"Yessum," Martha said meekly. "But I was only telling you God's own truth, Miss Lucyanne, and it don't look like there'd be no harm in saying that."

"Well, I've heard enough. If you can't stop talking like that, you can leave."

"Yessum," she said.

Lucyanne went towards the cabin door, stopping halfway uncertainly as though she could not make up her mind what to do. While she stood there, she heard Grady's drawling laughter inside. She turned around to motion to Martha, but Martha had disappeared. As soon as she realized she was alone she became frightened and her whole body shook convulsively. Grady laughed again, easily and unrestrained. The far-away sound of the guitar sounded mocking and taunting.

While she stood there wondering what to do, she heard Sallie John's gay laughter, and her whole being tightened with anger. Neither Sallie John nor any other woman had the right to be so close to Grady, because Grady belonged to her, and she wanted him now more than she ever had before. She knew if she could get her hands on Sallie John she would fight to get him back. She had never felt like that before.

Determinedly she began searching all around her for a stone, a stick—for anything she could use to drive Sallie John away. There was not even a piece of broken brick in the bare sandy yard. In desperation she tried to pull a fence post from the ground, but she soon found she lacked the strength to do that, and she ran to the cabin door and began beating on it with her fists. The frail boards rattled and clattered, but the door was securely latched on the inside. She kicked at it until her feet were hurt.

"I'm busy," Sallie John called out in a soft insinuating voice. "Stop that bothering me now while I'm busy entertaining."

Lucyanne beat against the door more frantically than before.

"Get away from there!" she heard Grady say, gruff and commanding.

The sound of Grady's voice made her catch her breath. She became absolutely certain that he was in the cabin when she heard him speak. She had fervently hoped that Martha was wrong and that somebody else was in the cabin. Now that she had actually heard him speak, she knew he was there.

"Who do you think that was, Sallie John?" she heard Grady ask.

"Some fool knocking on the wrong door," Sallie John said with a laugh. "Everybody around here in his right mind knows what I've got is strictly spoken for in advance."

Hearing Sallie John and Grady talking intimately to each other made Lucyanne take several steps backward. She was no longer sure that she wanted to go inside where they were. She stood in the yard gazing uncertainly at the crack of light over the threshold until she heard once more Sallie John's soft unrestrained laughter. There was no longer any desire to go into the cabin, but she did feel impelled to at least see them together. Going to the side of the cabin, she carefully pulled back the guano sacking until she could see into the room.

The instant she saw Grady and Sallie John she had a feeling of almost unbearable sickness in her stomach. What she actually saw was what she had feared and dreaded to think about for nearly a year, and now finally she was being forced to believe what her own suspicions had told her to believe and what Martha had tried, in her way, to tell her. She thought she knew now, even

though she still did not understand, why Grady
had avoided her all that time. The sickness in her
stomach passed away, but a feeling of complete
helplessness and despair came over her. She put
out her hand and clutched at the log wall for support, wondering what she would do if she had a
pistol. She shook her head. It did not matter now.
It was too late. There was no longer any desire
within her to hurt Grady or Sallie John. Something in her heart had vanished and she no longer
cared. More than anything else, she felt like
laughing.

Behind her in the night she could hear the tense
muffled voices of the Negroes, and she knew they
were talking about her and wondering what she
was going to do. That was something she did not
even know herself, but she did know that she
wanted to go away somewhere, anywhere. She
had to get away before Grady found her.

Turning away from the cabin, she began walking blindly across the yard. It was more than
merely going away from the cabin; she was leaving Grady. She thought she was being brave and
strong, and she had not wanted to cry, but when
she reached the path, she could not keep back the
tears.

When she passed the first group of Negroes,
she heard Martha calling to her, and she walked

faster. Then in the path behind her, she heard Martha's bare feet flapping ponderously and she left the path and began running across the field into the night.

"Miss Lucyanne! Oh my goodness, Miss Lucyanne!" Martha called after her, her voice wailing in the darkness. "Please, Miss Lucyanne! Come back here! Don't go running off like that at this time of the night! You'll get lost out there somewhere and I can't never find you again! Please come back here, Miss Lucyanne!"

She soon left Martha behind, and in a little while the pleading frantic cries could no longer be heard. Lucyanne had no idea where she was going and she did not care as long as she was going away from Grady and the Negro quarter and the great house and everything else that had come to be associated in her mind with him. In her blind haste she ran through a briar thicket. When she finally crawled out on the other side, her skin was scratched and bleeding, and her dress was ripped and torn.

She got to her feet and began running again. She was in a newly plowed field. Presently she stumbled and fell face downward on the ground. By then she was weak and out of breath, and each time she got up and tried to run, she soon fell sprawling on the soft earth. Finally, she did not have enough strength to get up again, and she lay exhausted and crying on the ground. For a long time she lay in the field crying convulsively and not caring where she was or what might happen to her.

Chapter VIII

Lᴜᴄʏᴀɴɴᴇ ᴅɪᴅ ɴᴏᴛ ᴋɴᴏᴡ how long she had been in the field when she heard a dog barking. Raising herself on her elbow, she looked all around her. She saw the hound clearly in the moonlight and she immediately lay prone again, hoping he would stop barking and go away. However, the barking became louder and more persistent, and when she threw clods at him, the hound, snarling and growling fiercely, began trotting in a circle around her. She was terrified when she realized that the dog was stealthily creeping closer all the time.

Somewhere behind her she heard a man's voice. One word immediately silenced the dog.

She sat up and looked across the field. Somebody was walking in long strides towards her.

There was only one thought in her mind then,

and that was that she had to get up and run before she was caught. She got to her feet and began
running as fast as she could. After going a short
distance she looked back over her shoulder. He
was only a few yards away. Screaming, she tried
to leap over a drain ditch, but she stumbled and
fell on the bank of soft earth. Before she could
get up and start running again, he caught her by
the arm with a firm unshakable grip.

"Don't! Let me go!" she cried frantically, fight-
ing with all her strength to get away from him.
The more she kicked and squirmed, the tighter
his hold became. "Please let me go! Please! Please!"

He was on his knees beside her and she could
feel his strong hands pressing her body against
the ground. When he bent over her, his face was
so close to hers that she could feel his breath
against her cheek. Once more she tried desperately to squirm out of his grip, but he straddled
her body with his legs and pressed his weight
against her until she was helpless. She closed her
eyes tightly when she felt him brush her hair from
her face with his hand.

"Oh, please don't!" she begged, her voice almost choked with terror. "Don't! Let me go!
Please let me go!"

"What's the matter?" she heard him say.

Lucyanne shook her head from side to side.

"Are you hurt?" he asked. His voice, she noticed for the first time, was kind and gentle.

She opened her eyes slowly and looked up into his face. "I don't know—I don't know," she said.

"I want to help you," he told her. "Won't you tell me what's the matter?"

"I don't know—just let me go!"

"What are you doing here?"

"I don't know!" she cried, once more trying to get away from him.

"You wouldn't be here unless something was wrong."

"Just let me alone—let me go! Please!"

"I know who you are," he said, smiling down at her. He turned her face upward when she tried to keep him from seeing her. "I wasn't sure at first, but I know now," he said.

"It doesn't matter who I am—just let me alone —stop holding me!"

"I can't let you go like this—Lucyanne," he said, shaking his head at her. Startled to hear him speak her name, she looked at him tensely, wondering how he could know who she was. "You've got to tell me what happened," he urged. "You may be hurt—a lot of things could have happened to you—Lucyanne."

She shook her head desperately, closing her

eyes and moving her head slowly from side to side.

"What are you doing out here in the field at this time of night? What are you running away from?"

While she listened to the sound of his voice, she stopped being afraid of anything. She no longer wanted to struggle to get away. The tenseness in her body went away and she felt weak and helpless.

"You are Brad Harrison, aren't you?" she said calmly. He could see her eyes open wide for the first time. "That's who you are, aren't you?"

He nodded but made no move to release his hold on her. Lucyanne wanted to tell him that she would not try to run away from him, but she felt too weary and exhausted to say anything. The next thing she knew, she was being lifted from the damp ground. Her body sank comfortably into his arms as he started walking over the plowed field.

They stopped in the path after leaving the field.

"I'm mighty glad I came out here to see what the dog was barking at," he told her. There was a slight trembling of her body when he spoke. She pressed her face more tightly against his shoulder. "If I hadn't come—" he said huskily. She looked up with a quick movement of her head, watching his face in the moonlight, but their eyes met and he did not finish.

The mournful wail of a locomotive whistle echoed in the night. Down below them in the patch of pines between the river and the slope a turpentine cup was set ablaze by the groundfire. Snuggling close to Brad, she watched the leaping yellow flame.

"I've seen you lots of times, Lucyanne," he told her with a sudden outburst of words. "I've been up to the big house to attend to the mules or something, and I'd see you sitting on the veranda or walking in the yard. Every time I saw you I wanted to say something to you, but I couldn't. Papa told me not to. When I go up there, Papa goes along. He's afraid Grady wouldn't like it if I said anything to you. He doesn't want us to do anything that Grady might not like."

The dog began barking again. Frightened, Lucyanne put her arms around Brad's neck. He called to the dog in a low voice, and he trotted back and stood at Brad's feet. Footsteps could be heard on the path not far away.

"Somebody's coming, Lucyanne," he whispered calmly, "but don't be afraid. Nothing's going to happen to you."

"But it might be him!" she whispered fearfully. "He might be looking for me!"

"Who?" he asked quickly. "Who's looking for you?"

"Grady."

"Something happened up there tonight, didn't it, Lucyanne?"

She drew a deep breath but made no reply.

"Something must have happened, because that's why you were down here in the field, isn't it?"

She nodded with reluctance.

"What was it?"

"I can't tell you."

"Something made you run away."

"Please don't make me talk about it now," she begged.

They both could see somebody in the path only a short distance away.

"It's Papa," Brad told her.

"Are you sure?" she whispered.

"It's him, Lucyanne."

Will Harrison stopped, gazing intently at Brad and Lucyanne. After a moment he came forward.

"Is that you, Brad?" he asked in a puzzled manner.

"Yes, Papa."

"What's happened, son?"

"I don't know," Brad replied. "I found her out there in the field."

"Why, that's Grady's wife," Will said in surprise. "What in the world!"

"We'd better take her down to the house, Papa," Brad said. "That's the best thing to do."

Will did not say anything right away. Presently he began shaking his head.

"Now, I don't know about that," he said doubtfully. "I don't know what Grady would say."

"I don't care what he'd say," Brad spoke up. "I'm going to carry her down to the house anyway so Mama can take care of her."

He started off down the path without waiting for his father. Will came along behind.

"Maybe that's all right, for the time being," he said. "But I wouldn't want to go against Grady too much."

Nothing more was said until they reached the house and went into the lighted front room. Brad's mother, Sarah Harrison, cried out uneasily when she saw Lucyanne's torn dress and earth-smeared body. She helped Brad put Lucyanne on the bed and ran to the kitchen for a basin of water.

"It's Grady's wife, all right," Will said with a worried expression on his face. "I'd recognize her anywhere. I can't quite figure out what she was doing down here in the field at this time of night, though."

Lucyanne closed her eyes to shut out the glare of light. Sarah hurried back into the room with a basin of water and a towel and began bathing Lucyanne's face and shoulders.

"Something dreadful must have happened," Sarah said with concern. "Just look at her dress—there's scarcely a shred left on her. The poor child looks like she's been terrified. I just know something dreadful happened to her."

"I think maybe I'd better go get Grady right away," Will said solemnly. "I wouldn't want him to think we'd take any steps without his approval."

"Likely as not, Grady Dunbar isn't even at home tonight," Sarah said with disdain. "It's a sin and a shame the way he treats this poor child —always going off from home and staying drunk half the time and goodness knows what else. Grady Dunbar is just like his father used to be, only worse."

"We don't have the right to talk about their personal affairs," Will told her. "What goes on up there at the big house is something we have no right to discuss, Sarah."

She glanced at Will with a meaningful look as she dipped the towel into the basin of water.

"Now, let me tell you something, Will Harrison," she told him. "I don't need anybody to give me the right to say what I think about Grady

Dunbar, because Grady Dunbar doesn't deserve a single kind word said about him, now or hereafter. And Mama Elsie Dunbar is no better than he is, either. She takes up for Grady no matter what he says or does. Those Dunbars up there—the blood Dunbars—are just not human beings, and I wouldn't mind being overheard saying so, either. Just look at this poor child! You can mark my word that she was driven away from up there by something Grady or Mama Elsie did! Just look at her!"

"Just the same, Sarah, we'd better not judge Grady too harshly until we know for sure what took place."

"Will Harrison, you'd try the soul of a saint! To hear you talk, anybody in this world would think Grady Dunbar owned you body and soul. You can let him own you if you want to, but I'm going to speak out as long as I have the breath to do it with!"

Sarah got up and left the room. Brad went to the bed and sat down beside Lucyanne. In a little while she opened her eyes and looked wildly at the room. He reached out and covered her hand with his.

"How did I get here?" she said excitedly.

Sarah came back with a dry towel and rubbed her arms and shoulders with it.

"Brad found you out in the field not far from the house, Lucyanne," Sarah said comfortingly. "We heard the dog barking, and Brad went out to see what it was. It's a mighty lucky thing he went, too," she added with a worried shake of her head, "because if he hadn't gone, you'd have caught your death of pneumonia out there on that damp ground all night. Besides that, goodness only knows what else might have happened to you."

Lucyanne saw all the faces in the room for the first time. In addition to Brad and his parents, several of the younger Harrison children, awakened by the commotion, had come into the room and were standing wild-eyed and curious at the foot of the bed.

"Now, maybe you can tell us what happened, Lucyanne," Sarah said kindly.

Lucyanne closed her eyes, squeezing them tightly shut.

"How did you come to be out there in the field all alone at this time of night?" Sarah asked kindly but persistently. "You mustn't be afraid to tell us."

Lucyanne shook her head, at the same time gripping Brad's arm.

"But you should tell us, Lucyanne," Sarah said. "Maybe something has to be done. And you mustn't be afraid, either. We only want to help you."

"I think I'd better go get Grady," Will said, shaking his head with concern. "He might not like it if I didn't go for him at a time like this."

"No! Please don't!" Lucyanne cried appealingly.

"What on earth!" Sarah said, looking at Will and Brad.

"I don't want to go back!" Lucyanne said desperately, looking from one face to another. "Please don't make me go back! You mustn't! Please don't make me!"

The Harrisons glanced at each other uneasily. Brad watched his mother's face.

"That's what you'll try to do—you'll try to make me go back—I just know you will! But I can't—I can't! Don't make me—please!"

Sarah hastily dipped the towel into the water and held it against Lucyanne's forehead.

"You won't let them make me go back, will you?" she said to Brad, turning and clutching at his arm.

"You mustn't talk like that, Lucyanne," Sarah said. "We're only trying to help you. All we want to know is why you were out there in the field tonight. If you've been harmed, something has to be done about it right away. Now, if you'll only tell us——"

"But you'll make me go back!" she said, sobbing. "I know you will—I just know it!"

Brad got up and went to where his father was standing at the window.

"Papa, she doesn't have to go back up there if she doesn't want to, does she?"

Will drew a deep breath and began pacing the floor.

"Of course, she doesn't have to go a step if she doesn't want to," Brad heard his mother say. "The poor child has a right to her own life. It would be a crime to make her do something that terrifies her like this. I'd be the last person on this earth to make her go back up there where Grady Dunbar is."

Brad faced his father in the middle of the room. Will's face was solemn.

"What do you think, Papa?" he said anxiously. "You won't make her do it, will you?"

Still saying nothing, Will left the room and went to the front porch. After he had left, Sarah took the children back to bed in the next room. Brad had not moved from where he was standing. In the silence, Lucyanne sat up nervously.

"Brad—" she said in almost a whisper.

He hurried to the bed and sat down beside her.

"What is it, Lucyanne?"

Tears were filling her eyes. She covered her face with her hands for several moments.

"Please don't let anybody make me go back," she begged tearfully. "I don't ever want to go back to that awful house as long as I live. I'd rather do anything else in the world."

"I don't want you to go back, either, Lucyanne," he told her in a troubled voice. He patted her hand tenderly. "It wouldn't be right."

"But he'll try to make me!"

"Grady?"

She nodded, and the tears began flowing in streams down her cheeks. He tried to console her by holding her hands tightly in his, but the touch of his hands made her sob more distressfully.

"You don't know him like I do," she cried. "He'll do anything—that's why I'm afraid of him!"

"I won't let anything happen to you, Lucyanne," he told her. "I'll see to that."

"But when he's angry, there's nothing he won't do. That's why I'm afraid of him—he'll do something awful—I just know he will!"

"Not as long as I can prevent it, Lucyanne. I'm not afraid of him. I'll take care of you."

She covered her face with the pillow and lay quietly on the bed. In a little while Brad got up and tiptoed from the room to the porch.

His mother and father were standing at the railing and talking in low voices. Brad went to where they were.

"I've never trusted that Grady Dunbar since the first day we came to this place to live," Sarah said, "and I don't know a single reason why I should now. I'm sorry we ever left the other farm and came here to work for him. It's the worst blunder we ever made, Will, and I'll never be happy until we can get away from here. He treats us the same way he does the colored up there in the quarter—like dirt. He's made you grovel so much that you've come to be afraid to draw your own breath without his permission. God in heaven never gave any man the right to lord it over other human beings the way he does us. That's something you've forgotten since we came here to work for him. But I haven't forgotten. I still know what it's like to call my soul my own, and I intend to keep on knowing, too. Now, if you're so afraid of Grady Dunbar——"

"We'll wait and see, Sarah," he said. "Grady may not be responsible for this after all. It might turn out to be something he had nothing at all to do with."

"Well, you can wait and see if you want to, Will," she said firmly, "but I don't have to wait. I said to myself the instant Brad brought her into the house that Grady Dunbar was in some way responsible. And I still say it and I still believe it."

"Anyway, we won't do anything till morning," Will assured her. "It's 'way past midnight already."

Without a word Sarah left the porch and went into the house, and Brad walked to the top of the steps that led down into the yard. Neither he nor his father said anything for a while. Will was gazing intently at the dark towering house on the hill.

"Papa—" Brad said finally. He stopped and waited until his father turned and looked at him inquiringly. "Papa, she doesn't want to go back up there and I don't think we ought to make her. I've been talking to her, and I know how she feels. It wouldn't be right to make her."

Will left the railing and went to the steps. He sat down and waited until Brad moved beside him.

"There's a lot of things to be considered, son," he said, speaking deliberately and slowly. "When you get involved with another man's personal life, you're treading on dangerous ground. Nothing but trouble comes to you after that."

"But this is different, Papa. She's the one who

said she didn't want to go back. Nobody ought to make her go when she doesn't want to."

"I know, son. But it's not our place to keep her away from up there if Grady says he wants her to come back. I'm older than you are, and I've seen——"

"That doesn't make any difference. If I had my way, she wouldn't go a step."

"I don't like to hear you talk like that, son."

"I can't help it, Papa. I don't want her to go back to live with Grady."

"What's that?" Will said in surprise.

"I don't want her to live with Grady."

Will looked at his son while his hands shook nervously. His face was troubled and concerned.

"That's a fearful thing to say," Will spoke up, at the same time shaking his head disapprovingly. "I hope Grady never hears you say such a thing." He continued to shake his head distressfully. "There's one thing I wish you'd stop and think about. She is his wife."

Brad got up and went down the steps into the yard. Still not speaking, he walked slowly out of sight in the night.

Chapter IX

After sleeping a few hours, Brad got up at dawn and ate breakfast. He sat in the kitchen with his mother and drank black coffee in the dismal gray light of the early morning. Both of them were tense and silent.

When he left the kitchen, he went to the front porch and stood looking for a long time at the gaunt great house on the upland slope half a mile away. There was no sign of life to be seen anywhere. Wisps of early morning mist began to rise from the damp freshly plowed earth and the huge fiery sun came up, bathing the bare fields and the lush growth of weeds and saplings in the hedge-rows with a warm rosy glow. It seemed as if in only a few minutes the cool spring morning had been transformed into a hot summer day.

Shortly after sunrise Brad heard his father leave the kitchen and go down the back steps.

He left the porch and hurried to the rear of the house, where he saw Uncle Jeff Davis and a young Negro field hand, Pete, standing beside a tractor they had towed from the field with a team of mules.

"What's wrong with that tractor this time, Pete?" his father asked.

"I declare I don't know, Mr. Will," Pete said, shaking his head. "I was disking in the upper field late yesterday when it just went and stopped."

"It's probably the gas line again, Papa," Brad said. "I'll take it down and see. Pete, open the tool-box and take out the wrenches."

Will and Uncle Jeff Davis sat down and watched Pete spread the wrenches on a square of oilcloth beside the tractor. Several field hands walked slowly past the house on their way to work. The sun was already well above the horizon.

"See anybody up at the big house this morning, Uncle Jeff Davis?" Brad asked as he bent over the engine.

"No, sir, I sure didn't, Mr. Brad," he replied promptly. A long period of silence followed, during which Uncle Jeff Davis glanced nervously at Brad and Will. "Mr. Grady wouldn't be up this early in the morning, noway, would he, Mr. Brad?"

"I thought he might get up a lot earlier than usual this morning," Brad told him.

Uncle Jeff Davis and Pete looked at each other with startled glances.

"What makes you say that, Mr. Brad?" the old Negro asked worriedly.

"Putting two and two together."

"How come you do that, Mr. Brad?"

"Just to find out things once in a while."

"Is that how you come to know so much, Mr. Brad?"

"That's one way, Uncle Jeff Davis."

"You sure is a smart white man, Mr. Brad," he said lavishly. "I reckon you know all about the goings-on up at the big house last night. Ain't no use for me to say different, because I was scared right down to the soles of my feet when Miss Lucyanne found out about Mr. Grady being in that no-account Sallie John's cabin. I told the Lord right then that I wanted to be saved from the trouble that I knew was bound to happen, because I know how the white ladies from the big house can tear up the patch when they find out what they didn't know about before."

"What did Miss Lucyanne do?" Will asked.

"The Good Lord sure did answer my prayer that time, because there wasn't no shooting or nothing like that at all, like there used to be when

Mr. Grady's daddy was in his prime and got caught messing around in the quarter. Miss Lucy-anne just run off, and that's all. Don't nobody know where she's at, though."

"She's right there in the house," Will told him.

"I sure am glad to hear that," Uncle Jeff Davis said, relieved. "I didn't want no harm to come to her. I been scared ever since last night that Mr. Grady might take it into his head to take it out on us colored, if something bad happened to her. Mr. Grady's a fine white gentleman, but he just don't like the colored. Looks like he just naturally don't like my kind of people, excepting when he takes a shine to Sallie John and her kind."

He stopped and waited to see if Will gave any signs of disapproving of what he was saying. Will's face was without expression.

"I don't like to say anything bad about Mr. Grady," Uncle Jeff Davis said, taking heart, "but sometimes I think maybe he tries to make things hard for me. I'm going on 'way past sixty and I sure do want to make a change before it's too late. I was born on this plantation and I've worked all my life for Mr. Grady and his daddy before him, and now I ain't got much more time to live and me and my wife hate to see ourselves pass away right here on this here same old place where we've always been. My boy Sammy's got himself a good-paying job at the saw mill in Maguffin and he say he wants me and his mother to come to town and live with him. I can't do the hard day's work I used to could, and I'd sure like to take it easy from now on while I'm still alive and able."

"What did Mr. Grady say when you said you wanted to leave?" Will asked him.

"He say I had to pay him money."

"How much money?"

"It don't make no difference, Mr. Will, because it'd be the same iffen it was five cents or five dollars, because you know as well as I does that I ain't got narry penny to my name. My boy Sammy might could pay it for me, iffen it wasn't so much, but Mr. Grady wants more than Sammy's got."

"If I was you, Uncle Jeff Davis," Will told him with a solemn shaking of his head, "I wouldn't do anything Mr. Grady didn't want you to do. You know yourself that a colored man can't afford to disobey a white man. They don't stand for things like that. This here's a white man's country, and you know it. If you want to leave, you get the money to pay him first."

"What you say is the awful truth, Mr. Will. I know that when I hear it. Everybody knows what happened the last time somebody up and left the place. Henry Crawford and his folks, who lived up there in the quarter in the cabin next to me, up and went, and Mr. Grady got the law after Henry, and they caught him with the bloodhounds, and the judge sent Henry to the work gang for ten years. Mr. Grady said Henry owed him nine years' house rent, seventy dollars for busting up a gang-plow, two hundred dollars for furnishing peas and fatback, I don't remember how much for letting a mule run away and kill himself butting his head against an old pine tree, and I don't know what all else. But it was heaps and heaps of money just the same. Now you know good and well, Mr. Will, iffen Mr. Grady's got me down on the books like that, I wouldn't never get myself paid out of debt to him iffen I lives to be two hundred years old, or more."

"You let that be a lesson to you, Uncle Jeff Davis," Will told him. "You stay right where you are, unless your boy gets enough money to pay Mr. Grady."

"Sammy said he'd talked to a lawyer in Maguffin about it, but I don't know iffen anything'll ever come of it or not. The white folks sort of keep the same mind when it's about things like that. Looks like somebody or other always has it in good and hard for my kind of people. Sometimes I think it would've been better if the colored had never been born. They don't have nothing but trouble as long as they live."

"You shouldn't look at it that way, Uncle Jeff Davis. There's a lot of work in the world that a white man would have to do himself if it wasn't for the darkies."

"Yessir," the old Negro said in a low resigned tone of voice. "Yessir, Mr. Will."

Brad started the tractor and drove it around the yard several times. The engine was humming smoothly when he climbed out of the seat. Pete put the wrenches and the square of oilcloth back into the tool-box and drove the tractor across the field.

Uncle Jeff Davis untied the mules and led them up the lane towards the barn. Just after he had left, Brad and his father heard a horse galloping towards them.

They hurried to the corner of the yard. It was Grady on horseback.

"Now, son," Will said anxiously, catching Brad by the arm as he started towards the front of the house, "whatever you do, watch what you say to Grady. You don't want to forget who we are, and who he is. We can't afford to step out of our place. It doesn't take more than one wrong word to make Grady lose his temper, and you know how much trouble that can cause. Let Grady do all the talking he wants to on his own land. We don't have the right to cross him in any way."

They could see Grady pull up his horse when he got in front of the house.

"But she said she didn't want to go back up there, Papa," Brad said, watching Grady ride across the yard.

"I know she did, son, but——"

"And I don't want her to go back, either."

"I know, son, but——"

"Well, I don't care who he is. I'm not afraid of him, and if she wants me to, I'll tell him she's not going back to live with him."

Will gripped Brad's arm. His hands were trembling.

"Whatever you do, son, don't say a thing like that! We wouldn't have a place on earth to live if Grady made us leave here. I'd be ruined. Nobody in the whole state would hire me if the word got around that we'd spoken up against Grady Dunbar. Think of your mother. You wouldn't want to be the cause of having her turned out of house and home, would you, son?"

Brad was silent.

"Now, son," his father said quickly, "don't forget what I told you last night. She's still his wife."

Grady could see them standing at the corner of the house but, instead of coming to them, he led the horse across the front yard and tied the reins to the porch railing. As he went up the steps, Brad began moving towards him, reaching the steps as Grady entered the front door.

Grady was standing in the middle of the room glaring at Lucyanne in the bed when Brad stepped inside the door. Lucyanne did not see Grady immediately, but when she finally looked up and recognized him, she screamed. Sarah ran into the room from the kitchen a moment later.

"What on earth's the matter, Lucyanne?" she said excitedly. "What's happened?" Then she saw Grady standing in the center of the room. He was scowling at her. "Oh!" she exclaimed, and ran to the foot of the bed.

"So this is where you've been hiding out, huh?" Grady said to Lucyanne. "I didn't think you'd be far away."

He surveyed the room suspiciously. It was a plainly furnished room. It contained two iron beds covered with carefully laundered candle-wick spreads, a high dresser, two rocking chairs, and several straight-back cane-bottom chairs. There was an oval mirror over the mantelpiece, and a large wall calendar, picturing a man and a small boy fishing in a stream, hung between the fireplace and the front door. There was little else in the room, which was used by the Harrisons as both a sitting room and a bedroom. The carpetless pine floor was scrubbed white.

Grady took a final glance behind him and went to the bed where Lucyanne lay tense with fear. Grady was sullenly angry.

"What do you mean by running away from home and coming down here to hide?" he demanded. His face was flushed, but his lips were practically bloodless. Lucyanne remembered the time she had seen him knock a Negro down and beat him with a trace-chain. She knew how cruel he could be when he was angry. "Why did you run away?" he said, raising his voice. "Don't you know better than that by this time?"

Brad took several steps into the room and stood directly behind Grady.

"Where in hell have you been all night?" Grady said. Without waiting for her to answer, he turned to Brad's mother. "What's she doing down here in this place?"

Looking at him straight in the eyes, Sarah compressed her lips tightly. He knew right away that she was not afraid of him, and he turned upon Lucyanne.

"Why don't you answer me when I speak to you?" he said, reaching down and gripping her arm roughly. "Why don't you say something? What's the matter with you?"

Lucyanne watched him in intense fear. She did not dare look at Brad for help, because she knew anything could happen if Grady turned on him at a time like that.

"When I speak to you, I want an answer, and I want it in a hurry!" he told her, jerking her arm painfully. "I'd like to know where you ever got the notion that you could run away from me!"

He jerked her into a sitting position and pulled the sheet from her. She was wearing one of Sarah Harrison's plain white cotton nightgowns. The torn and soiled dress lay on a chair beside the bed.

"Get out of that bed and go home where you belong," he ordered.

He pulled her to the edge of the bed before releasing her arm.

"Please don't hurt me!" Lucyanne begged, unable to stand the pain.

"You'll be begging a lot better than that before I'm through with you," he told her. "I'm going to teach you a lesson you won't forget in a hurry. You can't run away from me and not pay for it. That's something I won't stand for."

"Please don't say that, Grady!" she cried. "You mustn't hurt me!"

"Shut up! I'll say what I please, and I'll do what I please! Nobody's going to make a fool out of me and get away with it!"

While he was talking, Will Harrison walked

into the room. He appeared to be calm and undisturbed by what he had heard as he came through the door. Grady turned around.

"Good morning, Grady," Will said in a friendly manner. "How are you today?"

Grady nodded but made no reply.

"I saw you ride up a few minutes ago," Will said, "but I didn't know if you wanted to see me or not. Then I thought I'd better come in the house and find out if there was anything you wanted me to do."

Grady nodded his head at Lucyanne.

"How long has she been here?" Grady asked him.

"She came during the night, Grady. About midnight or later, I'd judge. Now, of course, I didn't have a thing in the world to do with it, Grady. You know me well enough to know that I wouldn't be a party to something that you didn't approve of. She came here, and we took her in out of the night. I thought that was the right thing to do."

"What did she come here for?" Grady asked suspiciously.

"I just don't know, Grady. She wouldn't say."

Grady picked up the torn dress and inspected it for a moment before dropping it on the floor.

"How did her dress get torn like that?"

"That's the way it was when she came here, Grady. Barbwire could have done it, or briars. There's a big patch of briars out there at the edge of the field."

"Women get raped in this country," Grady told him.

"They sure do, Grady," Will said, quickly agreeing with him. "Looks like they wouldn't go running around like that at night all by themselves, because you can't never tell when a nigger man might——"

"It's not always niggers who do the raping," Grady said, looking at Brad.

"You're sure right about that, Grady," Will agreed.

"Who else is there around here, besides him and the niggers?" Grady asked, nodding his head at Brad.

"Nobody at all, Grady," Will said quickly. "There sure ain't."

Grady was looking sullenly at Brad.

"Why don't you speak up and say something, instead of standing there with your mouth shut like a damn fool?" he said to Brad. "It wouldn't make a bit of difference to me if I thought you got her to come down here, or if a black nigger did it, because if I knew for sure——"

Grady swung around before finishing and glared angrily at Lucyanne.

"What makes you so quiet? What are you trying to hide? You'd better tell me!"

"Nothing, Grady!" she sobbed. "I'm not trying to hide anything. Honest, Grady!"

"Did you slip out to meet somebody?"

"No!"

"Did you leave the house by yourself?"

"Yes, Grady!"

"I don't know whether to believe you or not."

"Please, Grady!"

"If you're telling me a lie, I'll find out the truth, and don't you think I won't! You can make it a lot easier on yourself if you tell me the truth while you have the chance!"

"I've told the truth, Grady! It is the truth!"

Grady looked at her for several moments and then suddenly turned on Brad.

"What are you doing here, anyway?" he demanded. "Why aren't you out working where you belong?"

Brad glanced at his father, silently pleading to be allowed to say something. Will shook his head and stepped between Brad and Grady.

"Grady, I'll see to it that Brad makes up for any time lost. I wouldn't want you to think either one of us was shirking on the job."

"Why isn't he out there working now, then?"

"We've been fixing that tractor all morning. It broke down in the field late yesterday, and Pete and Uncle Jeff Davis towed it in for Brad to work on it."

"How do I know what he was doing last night?" Grady said. "That's what I want to know."

"You don't have to worry about Brad," Will said. "I'll see to that. Besides, he's a good boy."

"It would suit me a lot better if you got rid of him. Send him off somewhere. I don't want him hanging around here. I don't like him any more now than I ever did."

"But, Grady, he's my boy and I——"

"You're going to try to argue with me?"

"No, Grady," Will said meekly. "I wouldn't think of doing a thing like that. You know yourself I've always tried to do exactly like you told me."

"Get rid of him then."

Grady went to the bed and took Lucyanne by the arm, pulling her roughly part way from the bed.

"Now get out of there and go home where you belong," he told her.

"Please don't make me go, Grady!" she begged. She was sobbing, and tears filled her eyes. "Please don't, Grady! I don't want to go!"

"You don't want to do what?"

"I don't want to go, Grady."

"Well, I'll be damned!"

"I mean it, Grady! I mean it! I don't want to go!"

"Do you know what you're saying?"

"I know exactly, Grady!"

He slapped her face with an angry sweep of his hand, the blow knocking her on her side.

"That'll teach you something!" he shouted. "I don't give a good goddam whether you want to go or not—you're going just the same!"

Lucyanne looked beseechingly at Sarah. Before she could go to Lucyanne, Will put out his hand and stopped her, at the same time shaking his head.

"No, Sarah," he said in a low voice. "Don't."

"But, Will—" she started to protest.

Will shook his head again and pushed her away from Lucyanne.

Grady pulled Lucyanne from bed, picked up her dress, and threw it at her. She was crying helplessly.

"Put your shoes on," Grady told her, "and be quick about it. Don't let me hear any more of that talk about not wanting to go home, either. You're married to me, and you'll do what I tell you."

Will did not try to stop Sarah when she got down on her knees and helped Lucyanne put on her slippers. Will nodded to Brad and went to the front porch. They went to the railing and stood there listening to the sounds in the room behind them for several moments.

"Papa, you can't let him treat her that way," Brad said in a sudden outburst of words. "Can't you see that she doesn't want to go? You shouldn't stand for the way Grady orders you around."

"I've always tried to do everything Grady tells me to do, son, and one of those things is not stepping out of my place."

"Well, he doesn't own me," Brad said, slowly moving his head up and down. "I'm not taking orders from anybody."

"I hate to hear you talk like that, son. Sooner or later, that kind of talk brings on trouble."

"If you're afraid to speak up, I'll do it. Grady Dunbar's not going to make me scared of my shadow."

"What you say may be true, son," Will said gravely, "but just the same that doesn't give us the right to interfere with his private life."

"I've got all the right I need to go on," Brad told him angrily. "If he hits her again like he did a few minutes ago, I'm going to stop it."

Lucyanne and Grady, followed anxiously by

Sarah, came through the doorway. Grady took Lucyanne by the arm and pulled her across the porch and down the steps into the yard. She was crying brokenly.

Grady untied the reins and jerked the horse around.

"I'm not satisfied with all I know about her being down here," he said, glaring up at Brad. "But I'll find out. I'll make her talk."

He shoved Lucyanne towards the horse.

"Get on that saddle," he told her.

Chapter X

Lucyanne RAISED THE nightgown above her knees and tried to put her foot into the stirrup. It was higher than she could reach and, making it even more difficult to obey Grady, the horse sidestepped restlessly. Sarah, unable to stand by helplessly and do nothing for her, ran back into the house, closing the door behind her. Will, ill at ease, looked down at the ground.

"You're not wasting my time," Grady told her. "I can stay here all day."

She looked around briefly at Will and Brad, barely recognizing them through her tears.

"If you knew what's good for you, you'd get on that horse like I told you," Grady said.

Brad went slowly down the steps and stood in the yard. Grady watched him from the corners of his eyes.

"I just can't reach it, Grady," Lucyanne cried. "Don't you see, Grady?"

Instead of answering, he shoved her against the side of the horse. Whimpering pathetically like a little girl, she pulled up the gown again and tried to reach the stirrup. As she did so, the horse stepped backward and she lost her footing and fell on the ground.

"That's the way to do it," Grady said, laughing sarcastically. He made no move to help her to her feet. "Just keep on being a show-off and see what it gets you. I know you're trying to make a fool out of me. I can stand it a lot longer than you can. When you've had enough of it, get up off that ground and get on the horse like I told you in the first place. You're not making a monkey out of me."

Before Grady had finished speaking, Brad had started to Lucyanne. He got down beside her and lifted her to her feet. While he was bending over her, Grady kicked him viciously with all his might. The blow almost knocked him over, but he kept his balance and led Lucyanne to the horse and placed her hands on the saddle so she could support herself. Then he turned and faced Grady, more angry than he had ever been before in his life. Grady was laughing derisively.

"What's the matter with you—are you yellow?"

Grady said in a taunting manner. "Why don't you fight if you don't like it?" While he was speaking, his hand moved to his hip pocket and stayed there. "I've seen your kind before. I know how to take care of you."

Brad glanced at his father. Will was shaking his head with quick nervous jerks.

"You keep your low-white hands off my wife," Grady said. "That's something I don't stand for."

Brad turned his back on Grady and went to Lucyanne. He started to help her into the saddle but, before he could lift her off the ground, Grady jumped at him and grabbed him by the shoulder. Brad knocked Grady's hand away with a sweep of his arm.

"I said keep your low-white hands off my wife!" Grady shouted in a rage. "You act like you think you're as good as anybody else around here! I'll brain you so quick you won't know what hit you!"

Lucyanne tried to get between them. Grady shoved her aside.

"I don't care what you say to me, Grady Dunbar," Brad told him in an even voice, "but you're not going to mistreat her when I'm here. If you hurt her just one more time, I'm going to do something about it. That's all I've got to say, Grady Dunbar."

Grady, surprised, stepped back. A contemptuous smile curled on his lips.

"The hell you say!"

"I mean it, Grady Dunbar."

"Who in hell do you think you are?"

"You know who I am."

"You're goddam right I do! I've seen your kind before!"

His face had become flushed and his lips trembled with anger. He spat insolently at Brad's feet.

"Since when did you start looking after my wife? How long has this been going on?"

"That's my business."

"The hell you say!"

Grady took a step towards him, but Brad did not move. When Grady saw that Brad was not afraid of him, he laughed nervously and shoved his hand into his hip pocket once more.

"So you've been heard from at last," Grady said lightly. "I was wondering why you'd been so quiet all this time and acted like you were afraid to open your mouth. You didn't want me to find out there was something going on between you, did you?"

Brad said nothing, but he continued to look Grady straight in the eyes.

"Now you want to show off in front of her and

make her think you're a hell of a big he-man, don't you?"

"Have it any way you want it, Grady."

"Well, suppose I don't like it?"

"That's for you to decide."

"I've already decided, and don't you think I haven't!"

"That suits me," Brad said calmly.

Grady moved his arm threateningly as though to take the pistol from his pocket and Will Harrison ran down the steps and tried to stand between them. Brad pushed his father aside.

"I'll take care of this, Papa," he said firmly. "I know what I'm doing. You stay out of this."

"The only thing you're going to do is shut your big mouth," Grady told him.

"You leave her alone, and I'll keep my mouth shut," Brad said.

"Then shut it up and keep it shut, low-white! You're not telling me anything. I'll do all the talking." He laughed derisively. "You're the first low-white I ever saw who didn't have enough sense to stay in his place when he was told to. You damn fool, you act like you think you're as good as I am!"

Grady started towards the horse but suddenly changed his mind and turned around.

"What's been going on between you and her?" he asked.

Brad looked at him but said nothing.

"Why don't you answer me when I speak to you? What are you trying to hide?"

"What do you mean by that?"

"I mean what it sounds like. You're not as dumb as you look. You know what I mean."

"I don't have to answer that."

"You will if I say so."

"Try to make me and find out."

Grady took a deep breath.

"You wouldn't be alive to answer, if I knew for sure," he said threateningly. "If I thought something was going on between you, I'd— I'd——"

Will Harrison stepped between his son and Grady once more. This time he faced Grady and paid no attention to Brad's attempts to push him aside.

"Now, Grady," he said solemnly, "you know I'm not the kind to go against anything you say. I've always done exactly like you told me, and I wouldn't forget my place, no matter what happened. If I thought my boy had wronged you in any way, I'd be the first to call him to account. I'd heap rather send him away if he'd done something you didn't like, than let him stay here and make trouble between me and you. You know me well enough to know I'm exactly that kind of a fellow, Grady. Now, as I see it, there ain't a bit of cause for all this squabbling——"

"You keep out of this," Grady told him. "When I want advice from you, I'll ask for it, and if I hear any more lip from you, I'll run all you goddam Harrisons off my place. Nobody's going to tell me what to do about anything."

"Yes, Grady," Will said, his head drooping in subservience. "I reckon I kind of forgot and over-spoke myself, and I'm sorry about it already. I sure didn't mean to say anything like that to you."

"You and him both had better watch your step from now on," he said, jerking his head at Brad. "If I find out what I think I will, there's going to be hell to pay. No low-white's going to make a monkey out of me and get away with it. That's something I can promise you right now."

"That's right, Grady," Will said quickly. "I don't blame you one bit for feeling that way about things."

Grady picked up Lucyanne and swung her into the saddle. Brad moved close to the horse where he would be in a position to help Lucyanne stay in the saddle if Grady suddenly jerked the reins.

With a quick movement, Grady jumped forward and shoved Brad backward.

"I'm going to get you," he threatened. "I'll get you if it's the last thing I ever do. I know how to teach you low-whites a lesson to make you stay in your place."

He jerked the reins, the sudden motion of the horse almost throwing Lucyanne to the ground, and started across the yard towards the lane. Brad and his father watched them in silence until they were halfway up the slope.

"I knew it was going to mean trouble when I saw you carrying Grady's wife out of the field last night," Will said uneasily. "It was the wrong thing to do."

"What would you have done—run up to the big house with your tail between your legs and ask Grady if it would be all right to help her?"

"Now, son, that's no way to talk to your own father."

"That's the only way to talk to anybody who scrapes in the dirt every time Grady Dunbar looks at you. I've seen you do it all my life. It makes me sick!"

Will shook his head sorrowfully and looked down at the ground for a long time. Brad was watching Grady lead the horse towards the house on the hill.

"I hate to say it, son," Will said at last, "but it looks like the only thing for you to do is get up and leave. If you stay here, it'll only mean trouble for me and your mother. Grady's not the kind to stand for a trouble-maker like you on his place. I've seen him do away with niggers for a lot less than this. The only thing for you to do is get ready and go away as soon as you can. That's the sensible thing to do. It'll put an end to trouble before it happens."

"I'm not afraid of Grady Dunbar or anybody like him," Brad told him. "Grady Dunbar hasn't got me cowed. If he pulls that pistol on me, I'll knock him down so quick he'll think lightning struck him."

"Don't get hot-headed, son. Maybe you think you can take care of yourself, but the longer you stay here now, the harder it's going to be on me and your mother."

"There wouldn't be any Grady Dunbars if it wasn't for you and all the other bootlickers like you. You can be sure I'm not going to stay here and be one of them."

"You're going away then, son?" he asked anxiously. "If you want me to, I'll explain to your mother why you left. You don't have to talk to her about it. I'll explain it to her so she'll understand. It'll worry her sick if you stay here any longer, because she'll be afraid about what Grady might do. She wouldn't want you to be harmed, anyway."

"No, I'm not leaving now," Brad said, looking his father in the face. "I'm not ready to go yet. There's something I want to attend to first."

Will, wondering, remained silent.

Chapter XI

I<small>N THE SWELTERING MIDDAY</small> heat they came up the slope to the great house under the tall red oaks. It was always warm at that time of year when the clear blue sky of spring became streaked with the summer overcast which gradually turned into the color of dirty cotton. In another month it would be blazing hot, and the air would be humid and sultry. Under the scorching summer sun, burning fiercely through the haze, the lush vegetation, which was now so green and luxuriant, would wither and turn into crisp curls of brownish leaves and stalks. There would be increasingly longer intervals between thunder showers, and by the end of the summer drought the earth would be parched and dusty.

Grady had not spoken during the long tiresome walk up the slope from the Harrison house, but he had frequently looked back over his shoulder in order to make sure that Lucyanne did not try to jump off the horse and run away. Jerking the reins peevishly, he led the horse across the white sandy yard to the side entrance. When he reached the steps, he jerked the horse to a standstill.

"Beckum! Briscoe! Where in hell are you—you black bastards!" he shouted at the top of his voice. "You'd better get here in a hurry, or I'll skin the hide off both of you! Beckum! Briscoe!"

Almost instantly the two small Negro yardboys, each about ten years old, came racing pell-mell from behind the house where they had been playing on the woodpile. Their tattered and ragged clothing hung from their chubby round bodies in shreds, looking as if it would disintegrate before they got there. There was little change in their appearance from one year to the next, the only noticeable difference being an occasional new patch of old material sewn into their pants and shirts. Their black kinky hair was kept clipped close to their round skulls.

Beckum and Briscoe had never been paid for keeping the yard swept clean of twigs and pebbles and for doing various other daily tasks around the house. They picked up cigarette butts and smoked them in the barn; they played under the veranda when there was company and looked for coins that sometimes fell through the cracks in the floor. They wrung the heads off pullets and plucked them for the cooks; they watched for bourbon bottles which Grady threw from his window and painstakingly licked the last drop of whiskey from them; and they tolled the big bell in the yard at dinner time and watched through the window while the meal was being served. Month after month they did dozens of chores faithfully and uncomplainingly in alternating spells of energy and laziness. They were always around the house from sunrise to long after dark, ready to do anything and everything because that was what Grady had told them to do. They were curious about what took place inside the great house at night and they often shinned up the big paint-peeled columns and watched Lucyanne or Grady in their lighted room for hours at a time.

The other household servants, the cooks and maids and washwomen, were sometimes paid their weekly wages of a few dollars, but not often, because Grady generally insisted that they take their pay in old clothes or a sack of cow peas or some discarded article from the plunder room on the third floor. Whenever one of the women protested against being made to accept a moth-eaten shawl or a three-legged chair for a week's work, Grady was able to silence her by threatening to have her sent to the county jail in Maguffin for not paying him the past due rent of several years' standing, which he would claim she owed for having occupied a cabin in the quarter. As a warning to all Negroes on the place, Grady from time to time found an opportunity to send one of them to jail. All he had to do was to claim that the Negro owed him several hundred dollars and was preparing to leave the county in order to evade payment of the debt. In Maguffin the court was customarily reluctant to accept a Negro's word in preference to a white man's, and the Negro usually found himself in the jail or on the work gang.

"Where in hell have you been all this time, Beckum?" Grady said, scowling and gruff. "Have you black devils been riding those shoats in the pigpen again?"

"Nosir, Mr. Grady, we ain't been riding no shoats lately at all."

"If I ever catch you in some devilment out there at the back of the house, I'll whale the day-lights out of both of you." The two yardboys were grinning innocently. "And the next time I call you, I want you to be here before I finish. I'm getting mighty tired of waiting for you to get here. Are you going to do like I said, Briscoe?"

"Yessir, Mr. Grady," Briscoe assured him, his lips quivering with fear. "Me and Beckum'll be here just like you say. We was only out there stacking up stovewood so it'll get good and dry like it ought to."

Grady turned and glared harshly at the other yardboy. Beckum's knees began knocking together.

"What do you mean by being so slow, you Beckum?" he said. "Why weren't you waiting out here to take the horse? Do I have to yell my head off every time I need you? What do you think I hire you for? If I ever catch you loafing on the job again, I'll skin you alive. And if you don't watch out, I'll take your job away from you and give it to somebody else. Did you hear what I said?"

"Yessir, Mr. Grady," Beckum said, trembling more violently. "I hear every word you say, and I sure ain't going to loaf on the job no more as long as I live, and please, sir, Mr. Grady, don't take my job away from me. I'd heap rather you do anything else but that. I sure do like my job fine, Mr. Grady."

"If this happens again," Grady told them, "I'm going to get me a couple of yardboys who'll stay on the job and do the work around here the way I want it done. I'm getting tired of having to hunt for you when I want you. If you don't take care, both of you will find yourselves back down there in the quarter with no jobs."

"Yessir, Mr. Grady," they spoke up in almost the same voice, "we'll do just exactly like you said."

"Maybe I'll give you another chance," he told them. "I'm too busy right now to look for more yardboys."

"Yessir, Mr. Grady," Beckum said, grinning nervously. "It sure is fine to do that for us this time."

"What have you been doing all morning, anyway?" he asked suspiciously.

"Mostly stacking stovewood and cleaning out the hen house and hoeing in the garden, Mr. Grady, please, sir," Briscoe replied.

"As soon as you take the horse to the barn," Grady told them, "get busy and find something more to do. Niggers get trifling when they don't have enough to keep them busy."

"Yessir, Mr. Grady," they said in unison.

He reached up and pulled Lucyanne to the ground. Then he handed Beckum the reins, and Briscoe switched the horse into a trot. The horse and boys disappeared through the barnyard gate.

From the corners of her eyes Lucyanne could see several of the house servants, one of whom was Sallie John, and all of whom were tense with curiosity, peering at her from the curtained dining-room windows. Humiliated, and feeling that she could never again look at one of the Negro women without remembering their snickering smiles, she wanted to turn and run out of their sight forever. Just then she felt Grady's stare boring into her, and she glanced around at him fearfully.

"Go to your room," he ordered her. Before she could move, he had caught her by the arm, and then she felt herself being flung towards the steps. She almost fell. "And hurry up about it," he added. "All this wasting time isn't going to do you any good."

Holding her breath, Lucyanne ran up the veranda steps and hurried into the hall. As she passed the dining-room door, she could see the women gaping at her.

Almost since the first day she had come there to live, she had felt uncomfortable in the presence of the Negro women. They treated her with respectful attention and no disagreeable word had ever been uttered by any of them, but nevertheless they made her feel that she was not, and never would be, as much a part of the household as they were.

All the way up the worn and uncarpeted stairs

and down the long wide hall to her room she could hear Grady's footsteps following her relentlessly. The great house was hushed and silent, and she was thankful for not having to face Mama Elsie at a time like that. Once she was certain she heard the excited but subdued voices of the Negro women in the downstairs hall.

Lucyanne ran into her room, knowing it would be useless to close the door, and fell wearily on the daybed. In a few moments she heard Grady's heavy footsteps as he walked through the doorway. He slammed the door behind him so hard that particles of dust fell from the cracks in the pine ceiling.

It seemed to her that minute after minute went by, each succeeding moment becoming more and more unbearable, while she lay there waiting to find out what Grady was going to say or do. Whatever it was, she knew it was inevitable now. She was helpless and completely at his mercy. She flung her arms over her face to escape as long as possible Grady's sullen stare. Without actually seeing him, she knew he was standing there looking down at her contemptuously.

"Let's get started," she heard him say in his arrogant manner. It was the same authoritative tone of voice that he used when cursing one of the Negroes who had inadvertently done something that displeased him. "I want to hear what you think you can say for yourself. You ought to be ready to talk by now. You've had enough time to think up the story you're going to try to make me believe. Speak up! Let's hear it!"

Lucyanne held her breath for second after second, trying desperately to think what she could say. Her mind, tormented, throbbed with pain.

"What a fine lady you turned out to be!" he said sarcastically. "And what a sucker I was to let you fool me all this time!"

Still not looking at him, she knew he was standing in the middle of the room a few feet from the daybed and looking at her with hate and suspicion in his heart. She realized for the first time how ruthless and cruel he could be. She was afraid of him now.

"It won't surprise me to find out that you've made up a story in advance," he said derisively. "Let's hear it. You don't have to act coy—I haven't got time to coax you. Now, what's your story?"

He pulled a heavy chair across the room to the corner of the daybed. Before sitting down, he caught her by the wrists and flung her arms from her face.

"Whatever it is, it had better be God's own truth, if you know what's good for you," he warned her. "If you've got any notion in your head that you can lie your way out of this, you'd better start thinking all over again in a hurry. I'm not going to sit here and listen to you lie to me. I haven't got that much time to waste on you."

Chapter XII

As SHE LAY THERE TREM-
bling before him, Lucyanne knew there was no
escape. There was nothing she could say or do
that would make him stop tormenting her. If she
begged him to stop, he would laugh at her; and
if she got up and tried to run away, he would
catch her and fling her back upon the daybed.
She knew now something she had never realized
when she saw him mistreating one of the Negroes,
and that was that it gave him pleasure to be cruel
to anyone.

Grady, eyeing her with gross delight, propped
his feet on the corner of the daybed, lit a cigarette, and flipped the match stem to the carpet.
She tried to bury her face in the pillow, but Grady
caught her roughly by the shoulder and turned
her on her back.

"Come on and let's hear what you've got to

say for yourself. I'm not going to sit here all day like a damn fool. You've stalled long enough."

She waited breathlessly, wondering how long she could remain silent before he forced her to say something. Grady raised his foot and prodded her with the toe of his shoe.

"You've had your fun—now let's hear about it. They tell me that when a so-called fine lady runs wild, she really has herself a time. Of course," he said with a short laugh, "I wouldn't be prying into your little secret if I didn't happen to be married to you."

He prodded her again with his shoe, this time kicking her with the hard leather heel. The pain sent shivers running through her body.

"If it's all the same to you, you can start by telling me what in hell you were doing down in that field last night." His voice rose to a high nervous pitch. "You're not too bashful to tell me the details, are you? We're all the same color. You can talk to white people, can't you? When I caught you down at that Harrison house this morning, you acted like you'd done something to be proud of. Why don't you speak up now?"

Lucyanne shook her head, trying her best to hold back the tears that were coming to her eyes. She could feel Grady's eyes watching her mercilessly. For one time in her life she wished she were dead.

"You're not thinking you're going to keep up this cat's-got-my-tongue game much longer, are you?" He paused, his breath coming in quick angry gasps. "I'll beat the truth out of you if I can't get it out of you any other way. You know that, don't you?"

"Please, Grady!" she begged appealingly.

"Now what's the matter with you?" he demanded. "Ashamed to talk about it? Too ladylike, all of a sudden? Don't want me to know you slipped out to meet that Brad Harrison down there in the field last night, and got yourself mauled in the fun? Those low-whites treat their women rough, don't they? Didn't know it was done that way, did you? Didn't know he'd wallow you in the dirt and knock you around a few times first, did you? You must have been pretty much surprised to find out how a low-white treats a woman—or do you think I should call you a lady, instead?"

"Oh, Grady—please!" she cried helplessly. "How can you say such things! Please, Grady!"

He sat up in the chair, taking his feet from the daybed, and watched her with a sneering expression on his face. She had never seen him so overbearing and cruel before.

"What kind of a trick are you trying to pull on me? Are you trying to give me the impression that you learned a lesson? Do you want me to think that after it's all over you are sorry you did it and don't think it was worth letting a low-white beat you up for? Is that what you want me to believe? Want me to think you wouldn't slip out of the house again?"

"Please don't say such things, Grady! It's not true! It's not fair!"

He was silent for several moments while he watched her, taking delight in her distress. He knew she was suffering. Tears were streaming down her face and her throat was choked with sobs.

"All right, then," he said finally, "let's hear your version of it, if that's what you're bawling about. Maybe your version will be something new. I'm the kind of fellow who likes to keep up with the times. I'd feel left out of things if I found out I was behind the times. There's nothing like having a wife who slips out at night to meet a low-white and brings back all the latest angles. Hell, maybe I ought to be patting you on the back, instead of fussing at you."

"It's not true, Grady—not a word of what you say!" She shook her head, trying to make him believe her. "You know I've always been truthful, Grady!"

He laughed at her agony, leaning back in the chair and filling the room with the sound of a mocking voice.

"Grady, you must believe me," she said desperately. "You must—you must!"

"You haven't told me anything yet at all. What is there to believe? Why don't you go ahead and tell me how it is?" His manner changed quickly. He was sharp-spoken and angry. "I've given you plenty of time to tell your story. What more do you want me to do? Get down on my knees and beg you?"

Lucyanne sat up and looked at him defiantly. An instant later she realized she was no match for his anger and cruelty. Her hands began to tremble again.

"What goes on when a fine lady sneaks out of the house at night and wallows with a low-white in a corn field?"

"Nothing like that happened, Grady," she told him earnestly. "There was nothing like that."

"You expect me to take your word for it?"

"Yes, Grady."

"Do you think I'm going to believe you?"

"I hope so, Grady. I want you to believe me."

"What'll you do if I don't?"

"I don't know, Grady."

She thought for a moment that he was going to relent, but his silence was deceptive. He began laughing at her derisively again, and she covered her face with her hands and cried brokenly.

"Like hell I'll believe you!" he shouted. "What else would you be doing down there—darning socks for me in the moonlight! Do I look like the kind of damn fool who'd believe that?"

Lucyanne bit her lips, not knowing what to say. She was afraid to say anything for fear he would accuse her of not telling the truth.

"I could tell he was making a play for you," Grady said. "Anybody with eyes could see that. Why else would he be trying to take up for you all over the place if he didn't expect to get something out of it? Hell, that low-white thinks you're a push-over for him now. He's down there right now waiting to make another night of it. Hell, after last night he thinks he owns you."

"No, Grady!" she managed to protest.

"I should have killed him when I had the chance. That's where I made a mistake. But I'll get him. I'll take care of him before it's over."

"You mustn't do that, Grady," she said, trying to appeal to him. "That's an awful thing to do. You'll be caught and tried for murder."

"What do you expect me to do—go around grinning like a damn fool while he's making a monkey out of me? Hell, I've got pride. Nobody's going to wallow in a corn field all night with my wife and get away with it. There may be some damn fools in the world who'd let you beg off for him, but I'm not one of them. I'll fix him, and it won't be long, either."

Lucyanne was terrified by his threat. She knew he would not hesitate to kill Brad, or anyone else, when he was angry.

"Grady," she said earnestly, leaning forward and looking into his eyes, "I don't know all the dreadful things you're thinking, but what you've accused me of isn't true—not a word of it! You must believe me, Grady!"

"Then why are you so anxious to take up for him when I said I was going to get him? Why don't you put the blame on him?"

"Because he didn't have anything to do with it, Grady," she said quickly. "I didn't even see him until he found me in the field and carried me to the house. Nothing else happened—that was everything. He would tell you that, too, Grady."

"To hell with him!"

"Then you've got to believe me, Grady."

"Why should I believe you?"

"You've never doubted me before."

"Before last night!" He laughed at her earnestness. "Wouldn't I look pretty swallowing a story like that! If I believed that, I'd believe anything."

"If you'd only listen, you'd believe me, Grady. You know I wouldn't try to tell you anything but the truth."

He leaned back in the chair and gazed at her with casual indifference. He lit another cigarette and flipped the match stem on the carpet.

"I've got a little time to spare," he said. "Go ahead and tell your story the way you want me to hear it."

There was a series of timid knocks on the door. Grady jumped up, annoyed by the interruption, and flung it open. Crouching timidly, with head bowed in an effort to make himself appear as inconspicuous as possible, Beckum stood on the other side of the threshold. The whites of his eyes, big and gleaming, revolved slowly as he raised his head and looked at Grady standing above him. When he saw Grady's stern expression, he stepped backward into the hall. The boy's lips moved, but he made no sound.

"Get the hell away from here, Beckum!" Grady shouted angrily. "You're always in my way!"

Beckum, trembling, took several short steps backward beyond Grady's reach, swiftly ducking his head when Grady raised his hand threateningly.

"Yessir, Mr. Grady," he muttered. "Yessir, Mr. Grady. I heard what you said."

He still did not leave, however.

"What do you mean by bothering me like this?" Grady said to him. "I didn't send for you."

"I don't aim to bother you none, Mr. Grady," he said timidly. "I don't never aim to do nothing like that iffen I can help it first."

"Then what do you mean by pounding on this door? Don't you know you'll knock this door off the hinges if you keep that up?"

"Yessir, Mr. Grady, I know that and I wasn't doing it because I wanted to bother you. I only done it because me and Briscoe was down in the front yard sweeping it off nice and clean just like we aim to do all the time when we ain't busy doing the other things like you told us to do when we ain't busy sweeping off the yard——"

"Is that all you came up here to bother me about?" Grady said. He stepped forward and struck at the boy's head with his hand. Beckum, accustomed to dodging quickly, drew his chin down to his chest and moved his head deftly to one side. "If I wasn't busy, I'd whale the daylights out of you, Beckum!"

"Yessir, Mr. Grady," Beckum muttered, "but if you'd let me tell you——"

"Shut up and get back down there to the yard and start sweeping!" he said impatiently.

Slamming the door, he walked back to the chair.

"Well?" he said peevishly to Lucyanne.

Chapter XIII

Looking at grady that day for the first time without love for him in her heart, Lucyanne wondered why she had ever married him. She could look back now over their life together and see clearly that he did not know what it was to be kind and considerate. As long as he lived he would be arrogant, cruel, and selfish. There would never be a place for her in his heart.

She had loved him once, and had loved him dearly, but she did not think that she would ever again have such feeling for him. For a long painful moment her body shuddered as she realized that she had been waiting with false hope all those past months for Grady to reveal some affection for her and that it was impossible for him to express something that did not exist. If he had loved her, she told herself, he would have been unable to hide it from her. As she sat there before him, her whole body stiffened with aversion, she became convinced that his only motive in asking her to marry him was his need to have somebody in the house to take the place of Mama Elsie when his mother was no longer alive to pamper his selfish nature. He had no capacity for love for anyone other than himself, and Lucyanne realized that she had only herself to blame for not realizing that until now.

Grady was watching her impatiently, his small cruel eyes staring at her through the narrowed slits of his eyelids, and she wondered what he would say if he knew the thoughts that were racing madly through her mind. She could have told him everything, but she had no desire to hurt him needlessly. They were still husband and wife, and she knew she could never bring herself to be perversely cruel to him. What she wanted most of all was to be able to escape.

By then she was likewise impatient, and she wanted to get the whole thing over with as quickly as possible. Grady lit another cigarette with nervous hands. Lucyanne tossed her head backward and shook the hair from her face.

"What did you do that for last night?" he asked, sullen and gruff.

"I just couldn't stand it, Grady," she spoke up

at once. "I just couldn't bear it. When I saw you——"

In spite of her determination to be frank and outspoken, she suddenly felt weak and helpless when she remembered what she had seen in the quarter. Even though she had made up her mind to leave him, the memory of seeing Sallie John and Grady together challenged her to fight for possession of him. She did not want him, but neither did she want Sallie John to have him. Grady watched her curiously, wondering what she was going to say.

"What's the use of my saying it, Grady? You know what I mean."

"How in hell should I know? Go on. It's your turn to do the talking."

She had been warned about this. If she had listened to her parents, she would not be sitting there now in the midst of her shattered world with her head throbbing painfully, because they had tried to dissuade her from marrying Grady in the first place. They knew the reputation of the Dunbars, as everyone else in that section of the country did, and they tried to convince her that she would never be happy with Grady by point-ing out that the Dunbar family had outlived its time by several decades and that Grady possessed practically every characteristic of Dunbar decadence. There were many similar families in the region; the Dunbars were not unique. All such families lived in varying degrees of poverty, their vitality depleted and, fortunately, were usually incapable of reproducing their kind. Some of the men, however, frequently found a perverse sexual stimulation in intercourse with a Negress, as a result of which there were increasing numbers of mulattoes and quadroons in the country.

Most of the old families still clung obstinately to their decaying and dilapidated manor houses and stubbornly maintained an outmoded way of life at the expense of Negroes and uneducated whites who were kept in some form of peonage by means of threats and intimidations. In the course of time such families died out like a decaying tree, but meanwhile, as though nature had become impatient with delay, violence frequently broke out and removed the remaining members of such a family overnight. That was the principal reason why Grady habitually carried a pistol. His father had been shot and killed by a nineteen-year-old prostitute he brought home with him from Savannah, and his grandfather had been shot to death in an argument with a river-barge captain over the ownership of a hogshead of bourbon whiskey. Grady's only uncle on his father's side of the family, Duncan Dunbar, was killed by a street-car conductor he surprised in his wife's room in a fashionable Atlanta hotel during the opera season. For a long time Grady had lived in constant fear and he hoped that by carrying a pistol he would be able to prolong his life.

Lucyanne closed her eyes momentarily, trying to ease the pain that throbbed through her head. When she opened them, the room was whirling dizzily around her.

"I went down to the quarter last night, Grady, and saw you and—and that girl. It was more than I could stand. I didn't believe you'd do such a thing—I still don't understand how you could." She stopped and drew a deep reassuring breath. The room had stopped revolving around her, but every object in it appeared to be askew. "I had to go away—anywhere. I didn't know where I was going, and I didn't care—I just wanted to get as far away as I could. I had no idea where I was going when I left the quarter—I just ran." Once more she stopped. Grady was leaning back in his chair and watching her glumly. She could look him straight in the face now and not feel afraid. "That's why I went away last night, Grady. I had to do it. The Harrisons found me in the field near their house. That's all."

Grady sat up slowly and leaned forward until

his elbows were resting on his knees. His face was flushed.

"What do you mean, you saw me in the quarter?" he said to her in an even tone, the slits of his eyes narrowing until they were almost closed.

Nodding her head slowly, she returned his gaze unflinchingly. She could feel her breath passing rapidly between her parted lips. The pain in her head was barely noticeable any longer.

"I saw you and Sallie John."

A frown came to his face and she could see him forming a word on his lips.

"Where?"

"In that cabin."

"Snooping around, huh?"

He gave a short laugh, but the lines of his face did not change.

"No, Grady, I wasn't snooping."

"What fancy name would you call it?"

"I was looking for you, Grady."

"Why?"

She was unable to look him in the face any longer. She lowered her gaze and tried to look at her hands.

"I was lonesome and I wanted you."

Tears had come to her eyes in spite of her determination not to let herself cry at a time like that. Sobs rose in her throat and she was unable to suppress them.

"You're a fine kind of a wife for a man to have," he said, unmoved. "How long have you been going around spying on me like this?"

"That was the first time I've been to the quarter, if that's what you mean, Grady."

"What made you do it?"

"You know why I did it, Grady. You know as well as I do why I went down there." She had to pause for several moments before she could go on. Grady was watching her coldly. "I had no idea I'd find you—like that. And then when I saw you and—and that girl together in the cabin—I just couldn't bear it. I'd never dreamed I'd see you and a Negro girl being as intimate as that. It was like some awful nightmare." She began to weep. "It was terrible."

Grady was silent for a long time. He watched her cry with stolid indifference, the expression on his face unchanging and stubborn. She waited for him to say something that would break the tension but, as though her suffering was the penalty he demanded, he purposely remained quiet. Minute after minute went by while she waited tensely for him to speak.

"Hell," he said at last, laughing with casual indifference, "is that what all the fuss is about? That's nothing to get upset about."

"Grady, how can you say that?" she cried out, moving her head from side to side unbelievingly. "Do you realize what you're saying? You can't mean such a thing!"

He laughed at her again.

"Hell, what's a little thing like that got to do with it? The trouble with you is you're too sensitive about those things, Lucyannie. You're no angel who flew out of heaven. You know the facts of life. Plenty of white men in this country keep nigger girls, and always have. Everybody knows that. You know it yourself. There's no real harm in it. It's just a custom, like a lot of things around here. Keeping bird dogs around the house is another one. Nobody ever made a fuss about such things until you came along. You've got a lot to learn yet, Lucyannie."

"No, Grady," she told him firmly, "you're wrong about that. I could never make myself feel differently. That's something you'll have to learn yourself."

He chuckled to himself and leaned back in the chair. His appearance was so boyish and his smile so disarming that she had to force herself not to look at him.

"I thought you were too smart a girl to try to

make trouble over a thing like that, Lucyannie. Just look at what you've done! You've gone and whipped yourself into a lather about nothing. One of these days you'll be sorry you behaved like this. If you'll stop thinking about it like that and look at it my way——"

"No, Grady," she said, shaking her head.

"Well, suppose I was down there?" he said petulantly. "What of it?"

"Why did you, Grady?" she said with concern. "How could you do such a thing?"

"What you don't know doesn't hurt you. You'd never have known about it if you hadn't been snooping around where you had no business. It's something you can blame yourself for, Lucyannie."

"That doesn't excuse you for what you did, Grady," she said. "I'd never knowingly share you with a Negro girl——"

"Hell, I don't need any excuse for what I do," he told her, his voice rising with anger. "Nobody's going to tell me what I can do and what I can't do. I live my life the way I want to live it. That's something for you to remember. I do as I please, and you'll like it!"

Sobbing, Lucyanne bowed her head. She felt completely crushed by Grady's overbearing manner.

"Well," she heard him say, "I guess it's just

something you'll have to get used to, Lucyannie."
She looked up and found him smiling at her and
it was all she could do to keep from subduing her
feelings and throwing herself into his arms. That
was what she wanted to do. She felt that nothing
else mattered at that moment. To have him hold
her and kiss her and stroke her with his hands
would bring an end to all these harsh words. She
moved along the edge of the daybed towards him,
drawn to him by an irresistible desire to have him
fondle her naked body in the same way he had
Sallie John's. It would no longer matter what he
did if he would only take her now. She leaned
forward expectantly, putting her hand on his
knee. "You could do that, couldn't you, Lucyannie?" he said lightly.

"Do what?" she said, catching her breath.

"Do what we were talking about. Get used to
things the way they are around here."

She looked at him, but she no longer saw him.
What she saw was Sallie John, laughing and
naked, standing before her in a mocking pose.
She put her hands over her face, squeezing her
eyes with her fingers in a frantic effort to erase the
vision from her mind, but it remained vivid and
unforgettable.

"No," she replied, broken with emotion.

"Sure, you can, Lucyannie," Grady said, smiling at her ingratiatingly. "It won't amount to anything in the long run. My dad took me down to the quarter the first time. He didn't think there was any harm in it, and he always kept two or three nigger girls down there. He raised me that way, and a habit like that can't be changed overnight. It'll wear off gradually. Anybody will tell you that there's something about a good-looking high-yellow that a white man can't resist, and once you get the habit, it stays with you. That's the reason I've never slept with you. After sleeping with nigger girls for ten years, you just can't switch to a white girl. The habit has to wear off first. You just wait and see if it doesn't turn out just like I said. And now that you know all about it, it's not so terrible after all, is it?"

She shook her head gravely. "I could never stand that, Grady. You could talk like that all day now and I still couldn't change my feelings."

"You think it over for a while, Lucyannie. In a few days you'll come around to my way of seeing it."

"Nothing will change matters now, Grady. Nothing you can say will do that."

"We'll see," he said, nodding confidently. "You're young yet. You'll learn."

He got up and walked slowly to the daybed. She was afraid he was going to touch her, and she leaned backward to get beyond his reach. She could feel his knees pressing against her legs and, a moment later, he was kneeling beside her and trying to reach her hands. With a quick movement, she squirmed out of his arms and got to the other side of the daybed. She knew that if he put his arms around her, she would give in without a moment's hesitation.

"What's the matter with you?" he asked in surprise.

"You can't do that, Grady."

"Why not?"

"Because you can't come to me from that Negro girl."

"You're talking like a stuck-up low-white."

"Her color has nothing to do with it. I'd feel the same way if she were a white girl."

"You're trying to pretend to be hard to get," he said. "I'm on to your tricks."

Shaking her head, she moved away from him.

"There's no use talking about it any more, Grady," she said resolutely. "I'd never forgive myself if I let my feelings be changed now."

"Do you mean that?"

"I do."

"You're my wife," he said quickly, "and you'll do exactly what I tell you to do. Now, get that into your head whether you like it or not, because that's the way it's going to be. I've had enough of that sassy talk from you."

She shook her head at him but said nothing.

"Now you start listening to me," he shouted. "I want you to stay away from those low-white Harrisons. If you don't know what'll happen if I ever catch you with that Brad Harrison again, you'll find out. You stay in this house. I don't want to hear of you leaving it again without asking me first. If you try it, I'll see to it that you don't forget a second time. Understand?"

"I don't want to stay here, Grady," she said determinedly. "I want to go away."

"What the hell are you talking about?" He crossed the room and grabbed her roughly by the arms. He shook her angrily. "What do you mean by that?"

"I've got to leave, Grady. I can't stay."

"Is that so?" he said, stepping back and looking at her from a distance.

"Yes, Grady."

"And you're telling me you're going to walk out on me? Is that what you mean?"

"Yes, Grady, if that's the way it sounds to you."

"You goddam——"

He slapped her face with the palm of his hand, the force of the blow knocking her backward on the daybed. He bent over and slapped her again. Her face burned and her head swam dizzily.

"The trouble with you is that you haven't had enough of that!" Grady shouted. "I should have started knocking some sense into you when you came here! Nobody's going to talk to me like that and get away with it!"

He grabbed her by the collar of the gown and jerked her into a sitting position. The cloth ripped, baring her shoulders. She tried to cover herself, but Grady knocked her hand away.

"Now," he said, his lips curling, "do you still want to say it?"

She looked at him and nodded. He immediately knocked her down by slapping her face. Her eyes filled with tears.

"You're not going anywhere," he told her. "You're here to stay. I'll see to that. If you try to slip out and run away, I'll find you and bring you back. And if you think that slapping was hard, just try running off and see what kind you'll get when I catch you. I've heard enough of this back-talk and I don't want to hear any more out of you. You talk like you've never been married to me. Now, shut up before I get mad."

"That's not going to stop me, Grady," she told him. "Threats won't make me change my mind.

You have no right to force me to stay here. You can beat me all day, and I still won't change my mind."

There was a soft tapping on the door again. Grady ignored it at first, but after the tapping had been repeated several times, he turned around and faced the door.

"Who's that?" he yelled.

There was no reply, but soon the knocking began again. Grady strode across the room and threw the door open. It was Beckum once more. The boy was frightened and timorous. When he saw Grady glaring at him, he retreated awkwardly to the middle of the hallway.

"Didn't I tell you to stay away from here?" Grady said. "Didn't you hear what I said, Beckum?"

Beckum, his teeth chattering with fear, nodded his head with a jerky motion.

"Yessir, Mr. Grady, but——"

"Are you trying to bother me because you know I'm busy? Is that your devilish notion?"

"Nosir, Mr. Grady, but——"

"Then why can't you keep away from here and let me alone?"

"I sure will do just that, Mr. Grady, but I sure do wish you'd let me say what I come up to say first."

"Say it and get the hell out of here!"

Beckum swallowed hard. His teeth stopped chattering, but his knees began to knock together.

"Me and Briscoe was down in the front yard sweeping it off nice and clean just like we aim to do all the time when we ain't too busy doing all them other little things like you told us——"

"I heard that the first time," Grady shouted with impatience. "What do you mean by coming up here and saying the same thing over again!"

"I ain't got but one thing to tell you, Mr. Grady, and that's all I want to say, please, sir. Me and Briscoe——"

"Go ahead—go ahead!"

"Me and Briscoe, we was down in the front yard sweeping it off nice and clean just like we always aim to do all the time—" He stopped and glanced up at Grady's face. "While we was doing that, a white man drove up in his big car and stopped it in the driveway out there. He called me and Briscoe to come over where he sat and told us to tell you he wants to see you, please, sir, Mr. Grady. That's why I came up here and bothered you like I done the first time, and ever since then the white man out there in his car keeps on making me come back up here and say he wants to see you. It ain't my fault none at all that I had to come up here and bother you, please, sir, Mr. Grady, but the white man, he say——"

"What does he want?"

"He won't say nothing about that at all, except about wanting to see you."

"Who is he?"

"He say his name is Mr. Skeeter Wilhite."

Grady was both surprised and angry. "That goddam—" he said, stopping and glancing down the hall in the direction of the stairway as though he expected to see Skeeter standing there. He looked down at Beckum again. "How long has he been waiting, Beckum?" he asked soberly.

"Back since the first time I came up here and tried to tell you about him, Mr. Grady. It ain't my fault, Mr. Grady. I didn't want to come up here and tell you, but he made me do it."

"All right," Grady said, waving him away. "Get on out of here now."

Beckum raced down the hall towards the stairway as Grady slowly closed the door. After closing it, he stood with his back against it for a while. Still saying nothing, he went past Lucyanne, opened the wide veranda doors, and looked down into the yard at Skeeter Wilhite's big black sedan in the driveway.

"Grady, what's the matter?" Lucyanne asked him.

He shook his head, saying nothing. He did not want to see Skeeter Wilhite, and it made him angry to see Skeeter's car in front of the house. Grady knew what he wanted. Skeeter wanted money. So far, Skeeter had always trusted him until he could go to the bank in Maguffin and mortgage some more of the land, but this time Skeeter had won twenty-five hundred dollars, and he had let it be known that twenty-five hundred was more money than he was willing to trust a Dunbar for. Grady had promised to raise the money and give it to him not later than noon that day. He had forgotten all about it during the excitement of the morning, noon had passed, and it was now after two o'clock in the afternoon.

Grady had been losing money steadily at Skeeter's place for two years, and the time had come when he could not only not afford to lose it, but could not raise it, either. Skeeter was a shrewd and quick-witted gambler who knew the time was coming when Grady would be unable to raise a single dollar, and he intended getting all that he possibly could from Grady in the quickest possible time. Skeeter had made a lot of money in a little more than two years at his gambling house and bar just outside the city limits of Maguffin. Grady himself had spent almost fifty thousand dollars at Skeeter's place during that time, and several other men in the county had spent equally as much. Whenever the charge was made that Skeeter's games were crooked, he promptly increased the amount of money he paid out each month for protection. To be on the safe side, he carried an automatic in an armpit holster under the coat of his two-hundred-dollar suits.

Grady left the veranda doors and walked back into the room. He paced the floor nervously.

Presently he stopped in front of Lucyanne and looked down at her helplessly.

"Lucyanne, I don't know what I'm going to do. I'm in a bad jam. I've got to get some money somewhere in a hurry." He nodded his head at the veranda doors. "Skeeter Wilhite's waiting down there in the yard for me to pay him, and I don't have it. I tried to get him to wait a few days, but he's out here to collect. I've got to do something, Lucyanne. Skeeter can't be put off. He won't stand for it."

He sank heavily into the chair, his arms dangling loosely over the sides.

"Have you got some money you can let me have, Lucyannie? I've got to get twenty-five hundred, somehow. The bank won't let me have any more."

"You know I have no money, Grady," she said

quickly, suddenly feeling sorry for him. "I've never had that much money in my life."

"How about telegraphing your folks in Savannah for it?" he asked hopefully.

"They wouldn't send it, Grady. Even if they had it, they wouldn't. You know that. They'd know why I asked for it."

He sat for a while saying nothing and staring blankly at the floor. When he finally got up, she could see how deeply worried he was. She wanted to run to him and tell him she would do anything she could, but she was afraid to let herself get close to him. Silently, and without looking at her again, he left the room and walked slowly down the long hall to the stairway. After he had gone, she closed the door and, crying softly, fell across the bed.

Chapter XIV

WITH NO OTHER WARNING than a sudden and violent rush of wind that twisted and tossed the heavy limbs of the red oaks, a thunderstorm roared up the river from the low country, streaking the black sky with fiery tongues of lightning. The storm shook the great house until it swayed and tottered on its foundation, the aged timbers creaking with a mournful sound, and chips of rotted shingles were ripped from the roof and carried away like scraps of torn paper. For a quarter of an hour a drenching rain fell in a solid sheet of water, soaking the house until tricklets of water were running in practically every room. Each time there was a hard rain the Negro servants ran through the house setting out every available dish pan, wash bowl, and slop jar to catch the drip.

As quickly as it had come, the storm passed

over, but for a long time afterward thunder rumbled in the distance and jagged forks of lightning stabbed at the horizon. The hot earth was left moist and steamy, and the humid air was saturated with the clinging odor of rain-crushed peach blossoms. A raincrow cawed dismally from a persimmon tree in the field.

The sun had set during the storm and it was dark when Lucyanne finally got up and went into the bathroom. She lay in the tub and allowed the water to run until it reached her chin. While she lay there she tried to keep from thinking about what she was going to do or what was going to become of her. She was afraid of Grady and she hated the dismal house, but at the same time she was ashamed to go back home to her mother and father and have them know that her marriage was a complete failure. They would be kind and considerate and they would refrain from talking about the past, but her presence there would be a continual reminder of what had happened. By carefully planning her escape she knew she could walk out of Grady's life forever and disappear in the world, but she disliked to think that she would become one of the thousands of homeless girls who lived precariously by day or by night. There was only one other choice she could make, and that was to stay there for the remainder of her life. In that case she would have to succumb to Grady's will, like all wives in the family before her had finally succumbed to the Dunbar will.

She heard a noise somewhere in the house and she turned on the lights and quickly dried herself. When she opened the door and ran out, she was startled to find that somebody had already turned on the lights in the bedroom. She was not surprised, however, when she turned and found Mama Elsie sitting in the large chair and gazing at her in reproachful silence. Lucyanne had known all that time that sooner or later she would have to face and endure the inevitable scorn of Grady's mother, and until that moment she had been able to keep from thinking of the ordeal.

Mama Elsie, wearing one of her faded and billowy lavender silk dresses, surveyed Lucyanne contemptuously from head to toe, saying nothing until Lucyanne found a dressing gown and hastily covered herself. She could see Mama Elsie's fingers impatiently tapping the arms of the chair, which she knew by past experience was a certain sign of an impending outburst of abuse. Lucyanne avoided Mama Elsie's staring eyes as long as possible.

"Well!" Mama Elsie said at last. "What on earth have you been up to? What possible excuse can you offer for behaving the way you did? What possessed you? Have you no shame?"

Lucyanne drew the gown tightly around her and sat down on the daybed. Mama Elsie, her thin lips tightening, regarded Lucyanne with a scornful glance.

"I'm thoroughly shocked, to say the least, but not one bit surprised," she went on. "I should have known what to expect of somebody who practically came off the streets as you did. You had no right to take advantage of Grady's weakness as a man and use your body to entice him into marriage. It won't do you a bit of good to shake your head like that, because you know it's true. I can recognize the tactics of a whore when I see them flaunted in my face. Nothing so mortifying has ever happened in our family before and it's a disgrace we'll never be able to live down. I knew the first time I laid eyes on you that you were just what you are. You tricked my poor innocent boy into marrying you, because he was too much of a gentleman to send you back to the streets with the rest of your kind. If you'd had the slightest shred of decency in you, you'd have never taken advantage of his gentlemanly consideration. But no! Your kind lives by trickery! It was an evil fate that took my poor son to Savannah and thrust him into your path. The same thing

happened to his father in Savannah. There're no
good women in that awful sinkhole—they're all
shameless whores. God have mercy on me!"

"That's not true, Mama Elsie! I've done nothing to be ashamed of!"

"Nothing to be ashamed of! God have mercy on
me! Surely you don't believe for one instant that
you're fooling me with your pretended innocence!"

"I can't help what you think about me, Mama
Elsie, but you must believe me when I say I've
done nothing wrong."

"Nothing wrong! Grady told me everything!"

Lucyanne waited, knowing there was no way
of escaping Mama Elsie's wrath. It was something
that had to be endured.

"Even if you do pretend to have renounced
your previous life, which I don't for one moment
believe, you have failed to show the slightest consideration for me, or for anybody else, but especially for my son. Grady always has been a fine,
upstanding, righteous boy, and he is the one person on this earth who doesn't deserve such shame
and humiliation. I've never felt so sorry for the
poor boy in all my life. You slipping out and going off goodness-knows-where in the middle of
the night and meeting that contemptible low-
white Harrison in a vile and brazen orgy of sin!
Why, you behaved like you were back in that sin-

ful city carrying on your shameless enticement of
men! How can Grady keep the respect of his
tenants when his wife disgraces him behind his
back at night! No Dunbar woman has ever behaved in such an outrageous manner before in the
long and noble history of our family. What will
people think of us now? What will they say about
me behind my back? The shame of it! I'll never
be able to hold up my head in the presence of
good people again. It's bad enough to be afflicted
with a daughter-in-law who's nothing but a common whore from Savannah, but it's unbearable to
have you flaunt your lewd behavior in my face.
God have mercy on me!"

Lucyanne wanted to cry, but she knew she had
to do everything she could to convince Mama
Elsie that she had done no wrong, and she realized
that tears at a time like that would appear to be
an admission of guilt.

"I don't know what Grady told you, Mama
Elsie," she said tensely, "but all I did was leave
the house and go across the field last night. Nothing else happened. Please believe me. I'm telling
you the truth. The Harrisons found me and took
me to their house. I just couldn't stand it here any
longer. I couldn't stay. I had to leave. Grady——"

"I don't have the slightest idea what you're
talking about, young woman, but I'm Grady's

mother and I will not allow you or anybody else to think you can turn me against my own son. Grady is a good boy, and I won't stand having him blamed for your sins. I never wanted Grady to marry in the first place, and most certainly not to marry you or one of your kind. I'm perfectly able to take care of Grady, and if you lived here a hundred years, you'd never be able to take my place in his affections. Any creature who would do what you did last night——"

"But it was Grady's fault, Mama Elsie!" Lucyanne said steadfastly. "If Grady hadn't——"

"No! I won't listen to a word of it! It's bad enough for you to run away and be found half-naked with that young low-white Harrison, but it's even worse for you to sit there and try to say Grady is to blame. No! I won't believe a single, solitary word of it! You can just save your breath if that's what you've made up your mind to say. If Grady had listened to me, I wouldn't be here now with this shame hanging over me, because I begged him not to marry anybody. I knew something like this would happen. No woman on this earth could ever love him like I do. The poor boy has known nothing but misery and unhappiness since you came here."

"Did Grady tell you why I left, Mama Elsie?"

"I haven't the slightest idea what you're talking about, young woman."

"But he must have told you something, because you knew I'd been away from the house."

"As long as you persist in trying to blame my son for your brazen sins, I refuse to listen to a word of it. I am not interested in anything you say."

The door opened and Martha came in carrying a tray. With a shy glance at Lucyanne, she went to the table and began arranging dinner dishes. There was not a word spoken in the room while Martha was there. After she had finished, she tiptoed to the hall and noiselessly closed the door. As soon as Martha had left, Lucyanne wanted to call her back and make her tell Mama Elsie what had happened in the quarter, but she was afraid to do anything that might make Mama Elsie angry.

"Well, go on and eat your dinner," Mama Elsie said harshly. "You probably haven't eaten all day."

"I can't eat anything, Mama Elsie," she said, shaking her head. "I'm not hungry."

"It's not going to do any good to sit there and try to make a martyr of yourself, because I'm not interested in whether you eat or not. Acting like that isn't going to have the slightest effect on me.

You'll never gain any sympathy from me, young woman."

Several minutes passed before anything else was said. Mama Elsie watched her with a haughty and disdainful air as if to say that she had made up her mind that Lucyanne was guilty of an unpardonable sin and that forgiveness was out of the question. The fingers of her right hand began to tap monotonously on the arm of the chair.

"God have mercy on me! I don't know what's to become of our fine family name now, after it's been dragged through the mire by a complete outsider. I know I'll never be able to hold up my head after this. I can just see the smirks on the faces of people like those Harrisons down there when our name is mentioned. The whole aim in life of such people is to drag a family like ours down to their level. I don't know what Grady could have been thinking of when he married you. But I just know you tricked him into it!"

"Mama Elsie," Lucyanne said in desperation, "you've got to listen to me and believe me. This would never have happened if I hadn't found Grady——"

"You are the most perverse creature I've ever seen! You will persist in trying to blame my poor innocent son!"

"Grady was in Sallie John's cabin last night."

The old woman was dazed. Her mouth fell open and her eyes stared unseeingly at Lucyanne. After a while she raised her hands slowly and drew her fingers over her eyelids in a gesture of bewilderment. Her haughty manner disappeared completely and her round puffy cheeks sagged lifelessly.

"What did you say, child?" she asked weakly.

Lucyanne repeated what she had said.

"That trifling nigger!" she said. "That low-down prissy nigger-wench! God have mercy on me. I knew she was up to something. Her kind always go after the most aristocratic white man within reach. Never a day passed that one of them didn't entice Grady's father. But my poor boy! Are you sure you're telling me the truth?"

"Yes, Mama Elsie. You can ask Martha. She knows. She'll tell you the same thing."

"God have mercy on me."

Her huge body sank deep into the chair and she heaved a prolonged agonizing sigh.

"My poor, poor boy," she said in a low voice that sounded tired and despairing. "It was bound to happen sooner or later, because it's a curse, child." All pride had vanished. She was now a sorrowing old woman. Her thin lips trembled and she gazed helplessly at Lucyanne. "It's a curse of the Dunbars, child. The men of the family have always been drawn to those darkey girls down there like flies to molasses. Grady's father was afflicted by them, and no amount of pleading or inducement could keep him from them. And Grady's grandfather was even worse. He brought darkey girls right here into this house, two or three at a time, and kept them locked in his room at night. When I married Grady's father and came here to live, we spent the first night together in that room across the hall, and all night long I could hear those screaming naked darkey girls in this very room with Grady's grandfather. I didn't know what I had gotten into, but it wasn't long before I found out. It's hardly to be expected that Grady would be an exception. Some men take to liquor, some take to darkey girls. The Dunbar men take to both. God have mercy on me."

Her body shook and heaved and tears trickled down her wrinkled cheeks. She was soon overcome by a spasm of wailing that could be heard throughout the house. Lucyanne could not keep from feeling sorry for her, and she got up and went to Mama Elsie's side and put her hand on the old woman's shaking shoulders. Presently Mama Elsie looked up into her face and then, with sudden fury, knocked Lucyanne's hand aside.

"I know what you're up to!" she cried, hitting her chest with her fists as though trying to flail the anguish from her huge body. "God have mercy on me! I might have known it! It's your trickery again! You've fooled me into telling you what I know about Grady so you'll have an excuse to leave him for that low-white Harrison. That's it! That's your scheme! I knew it! You'll break Grady's heart—that's what you'll do. You'll cast him aside, just like any whore, when you're through with him. Now you're going to a younger man. My poor boy will have nobody to look after him when I'm gone. He'll be all alone in the world. And to think you'd do a thing like that to us—after I've treated you like my own daughter! I can't stand the thought of it—I can't endure it! It'll kill me—it'll send me to my grave years ahead of time! God have mercy on me."

She slumped deeper into the chair, throwing her arms about her head and moaning in agony.

Lucyanne got down on her knees before her and tried to comfort her. Mama Elsie pushed her away and stood up. She swayed on her feet for several moments.

"It's my heart," Mama Elsie said weakly, holding her hands against her chest. "This is more than I can stand. It's going to be the end of me. I'm going to die. Something tells me I am. God have mercy on me."

Unaided, she moved unsteadily towards the

door. Lucyanne stayed at her side until she reached the hall. With a sweep of her hand she motioned Lucyanne away.

"All I ask is that you wait till Grady comes back," she said in a pleading voice. "With my last breath I ask that of you. Please stay till he comes back."

"Where has he gone?" Lucyanne asked in surprise.

"He drove off towards town just after Mr. Wilhite left. He's probably got important business to attend to in Maguffin." She began wailing again. "If you never do anything else for me, wait until he comes home."

Tottering unsteadily, she went down the hall towards her room. After she had passed out of sight, Lucyanne closed the door and sank wearily into the chair.

Chapter XV

SOMEBODY WAS ON THE veranda. As soon as Lucyanne heard the slow steady squeaking of the warped flooring, she sat up in alarm. The sound was not like any she had ever heard before and she was certain it was not Beckum and Briscoe this time. Jumping up, she ran to the veranda doors and threw them open.

At first she could not see anything in the darkness, but while she stood there, frightened and breathless, the figure of a man slowly took shape as he moved towards her. She hastily stepped backwards into the room.

"Lucyanne, you look wonderful!" he said, coming towards her. "Lucyanne——"

"What are you doing here, Brad?" she said in fear. "You mustn't come in here!"

With a quick movement, he seized her by the arm and drew her through the doorway to the semidarkness of the veranda. Then he put his arms around her and crushed her body against his. She could feel his hot breath on her face as he searched for her lips. After he had kissed her, she felt too weak and helpless to struggle against him. The dressing gown had slipped from her shoulders and she could feel his rough hands stroking her body. The excitement and fear made her head feel dizzy and her knees suddenly gave way. Brad picked her up and carried her to the settee against the wall. When she opened her eyes, he was kneeling beside her with his arms locked around her waist. When she tried to push him away, he held her tighter.

"Are you all right now?" he asked.

She nodded. "Yes."

"I couldn't stay away, Lucyanne. I've done nothing but think about you all day. I just had to come up here to see you."

"But you shouldn't, Brad. If Grady or Mama Elsie found you here, they'd never believe a word I said."

"You said you didn't want to come back up here. What difference does it make what they think?"

"I don't know, but it does."

He moved closer, pressing his hot face against her skin. Her breath came in quick gasps.

"I want you to go away with me, Lucyanne," he said in a nervous husky voice. "Will you go away with me?"

She tried to push him away. "No! I couldn't do that! You mustn't say such things!"

"Why not?" he asked. "Last night you said——"

"I don't know what I said last night. But I couldn't do a thing like that."

"You don't think I'm good enough for you—is that why?" He looked at her with a faint smile on his lips. "Is that the real reason?"

"Of course not, Brad!" she told him quickly, putting her hand on his. She was afraid she had hurt him. "That has nothing to do with it."

"Then why won't you go with me?"

"You don't know anything about me, Brad. You don't know what kind of person I am."

"I know you're wonderful—and that I love you and want you."

"But you don't know what I'm like—or what I used to be before I came here. Suppose I told you that I used to be—not quite good. That I was a different kind of girl before I married Grady and came here to live. What would you think then?"

"I wouldn't believe it."

She laughed to herself for a moment.

"Mama Elsie won't believe I was good, and you

won't believe I was bad. I guess people always believe what they want to believe."

"I don't care what you used to be. That has nothing to do with the way you are now. You're beautiful and wonderful, and I love you and want to marry you. That's all that matters."

Shaking her head, she looked away from him. In the long silence that followed, she knew he was looking up into her face and she carefully avoided letting her glance meet the steady gaze of his eyes. Finally, he got up from his knees and sat down beside her on the settee.

"I know why it is," he said in a low voice. "It's because you live up here in the big house and I live down there in a tenant house. I might have known it would turn out like this. You're afraid to tell me the real reason. That's why you made up that story about having some sort of a past. Girls don't bring up things like that when they're trying to get rid of a man unless it's to cover up the real reason. Sure, I live in a tenant house. What of it? I'm just as good as you or anybody else who lives up here in the big house, and you know it. If I lived in one of these rotting old houses and loafed all the time and borrowed money to live on, you'd marry me as quick as you married Grady. Well, one of these days you'll be sorry, because you'll wake up and find out that you made a mistake. I'm going to amount to something in life, and I can give you a lot more than any other man will ever give you, and money won't be the only thing, either. If you change your mind any time soon, let me know."

He started to get up, but Lucyanne pulled him back beside her. Tears were filling her eyes and she was unable to keep sobs from rising in her throat. She sat still and tense with her fingers gripped tightly around his hand.

Down in the quarter one of the Negro girls was singing. Above the sound of the guitar, a clear plaintive voice drifted sonorously through the damp night. For once the music she heard was soothing and comforting.

> *Makes no mind what you wish,*
> *I'll always be your heapin' dish. . . .*

They sat there for a long time listening to the words of the seemingly endless song. It was long past midnight then, and one by one the lights in the cabins went out.

"You have a right to think anything you want to, Brad," she told him at last, "but it's Grady——"

"What about him?" he said stiffly.

"Grady's in trouble. I couldn't think of leaving him now."

"That's a funny way to look at it, after the way he's treated you." His voice was bitter. "You've got so many excuses I don't believe any of them."

"I'm still married to him. I couldn't leave him while he's in trouble. I'd never forgive myself."

"What kind of trouble?" he asked skeptically. "Did Sallie John run away?"

Lucyanne put her face in her hands and cried. Brad watched her uneasily, feeling helpless and trying to think of something he could say that would undo the harm he had caused. As soon as he had mentioned Sallie John's name, he realized how cruel and thoughtless he was.

"I'm sorry, Lucyanne," he told her. "I shouldn't have said anything like that."

She became quiet after that and rested her head on the back of the settee. "Please don't ever say anything like that again," she said quietly. "I can't stand it."

"I'll never do it again, Lucyanne," he promised.

"All right, Brad," she said. "It's all over now. Let's don't talk about it any more."

"Tell me about Grady. What kind of trouble is he in now?"

"It's money. He owes twenty-five hundred dollars this time. He doesn't have it, but he's got to find some way to pay it. I don't know what he's going to do. It's terrible."

"Who does he owe? Skeeter Wilhite?"

She nodded. "How did you know?"

"That's easy to guess. That's where all his money goes, isn't it?"

"I suppose so."

"Are you going to help him?"

"I don't have any money."

"Then why doesn't he mortgage some more land?"

"He did that last time—for the last time. The bank won't lend any more on this farm."

"Well," he said, "it looks like Grady's got himself backed into a corner this time. If he gets himself out of this jam, he's a lot smarter than anybody else who's ever owed Skeeter Wilhite money and got away without paying it. There's nobody tougher than Skeeter when it comes to collecting what's owed him."

Brad stood up. He looked down at Lucyanne undecidedly for a while, and then he walked slowly towards the stairway at the end of the veranda. Lucyanne watched him until he was almost out of sight before she got up. Then she saw him stop and quickly turn around. Neither of them spoke. Moment after moment passed, and then suddenly he ran to her and put his arms around her in a strong restless embrace. For the first time she did not try to resist him when he kissed her. After that she felt herself being lifted from her feet and carried through the doorway to her bed.

Chapter XVI

GRADY WAS WORRIED, MORE worried than he had ever been before in his life. It was after banking hours when he got to town late that afternoon, but he had gone into the bank through the back door and had had a long talk with Howard Phillips, the president. Howard had told him frankly that the bank would not consider loaning him the money because the Dunbar place was already mortgaged to the limit and because he had no other security to put up. However, when Grady was leaving the bank, Howard advised him to try to raise the money through his friends or, if that failed, to do his best to persuade Skeeter Wilhite to give him additional time. In their minds, though, they both knew that one was as impossible to achieve as the other.

After that, Grady had driven his car through the wide tree-lined streets of Maguffin for several hours that evening, at first racing through the residential sections of town, later going slowly up and down the main street time after time past the post office, the courthouse, and the Jefferson Davis monument, and all the time trying to think of some way to get twenty-five hundred dollars before morning.

At midnight he had finally gone out to Skeeter Wilhite's place, hoping that in some way he could persuade Skeeter to let him have more time. Grady had not forgotten that when Skeeter left him that afternoon, Skeeter's last warning was for him to pay the money that night without fail.

Skeeter's place, which was known by no other name, but which was readily identified by the Jax Beer sign over the entrance, and which was exactly three miles from the courthouse, formerly had been a public grade school. Skeeter had bought the four-room building from the county when the schools of the district were consolidated, and for two years he had been able to operate continuously and profitably by paying fifteen per cent of gross income for protection. No one was found who would say how the money was paid, or to whom it was paid, because that was a detail known only to Skeeter and Judge Lovejoy, his lawyer, but nevertheless his protection was secure and authoritative. Other aspiring gambling-house keepers, thinking they could get away with similar operations, found themselves hustled out of the county at the point of a deputy sheriff's gun and warned to stay out.

The former school building, innocent in appearance, stood in a grove of long-needle pines fifty yards from the highway. The outdoor basketball court, with its goal posts still standing, was used as a parking lot for Skeeter's customers. The grove itself, even when school kept, had always been a popular place at night, and there were usually two or three couples somewhere under the pines after dark.

Several times during the past two years the ministers in Maguffin, worried over dwindling church collections, had tried to drive Skeeter out of the county by preaching strongly worded sermons against gambling and roadhouses. Skeeter was never mentioned by name, but all who attended church services knew that it was he who was being talked about, and each time a sermon was delivered by one of the ministers against dice games, drinking parties in the grove, and the three waitresses who wore handkerchief-size black chiffon aprons, there was an immediate increase in Skeeter's patronage, and on the following Sunday there was generally an unusually large contribution in a plain sealed envelope in

the collection basket. Each time one of the ministers announced such a sermon-topic in advance,
there was always an overflowing attendance of
members and non-members alike who came to
hear in plainly worded detail his descriptions of
the antics of Skeeter's uninhibited waitresses and
of the erotic behavior of drunken young girls in
the grove at night, and the perverse effect was
that on Sunday nights following one of the sermons Skeeter's parking lot was jammed with auto-
mobiles until dawn. Later, the ministers com-
plained to the sheriff, but he declined to take
action on the ground that he had no authority to
meddle with a taxpayer's affairs as long as no
crime was being committed or when there was
no disturbance of the peace. After that, the ministers went to the county commissioners and
charged them with laxity of office for allowing
Skeeter to encourage slumber parties in the grove,
where half a dozen men and girls spent the night
together on automobile cushions or on pine straw
under the trees, but nothing ever came of that,
either.

When Grady reached Skeeter's place, he
parked his car on the basketball court at the side
of the building and went inside. There were several men sitting on stools at the bar when he entered the front room. Somebody called to him to

have a beer, but Grady declined and went into the back room. There were five or six men in a group at the crap table, and several others were sitting at tables drinking beer or bourbon. Grady walked past the crap table and then looked at the faces in the room again. Skeeter was not there. One of the men at a table nodded to Grady and, with a motion of his hand, invited him to sit down. Grady shook his head and went to the corner where he usually sat. There he had a good view of the entire room and could see everyone who came and left. He knew most of the men in the room. One was a pulpwood buyer for a paper mill, one was a state highway engineer, and another was the manager of the Maguffin office of the electric power company. Besides them, he recognized two or three of the courthouse crowd at the crap table. From time to time one of the men in the room turned around and glanced at him curiously, but he ignored them by pretending not to recognize anyone.

He had been sitting in the corner for almost half an hour when he looked up and saw Peggy smiling at him. Peggy was the tall dark-haired waitress and bar girl who always brought Grady his bourbon when he called for it. She was slender and shapely and youthful looking, and in her brief black apron, which was designed to be more

provocative than concealing, she was far more attractive then either of the other two waitresses.
She had worked at Skeeter's place for about six
months, but no one had succeeded in finding out
where she came from. Every time one of the customers tried to persuade her to tell something
about herself, she smiled and shook her head. The
other two waitresses, both of whom were thin-
lipped, blonde, and chubby, had resented her at-
tractiveness from the beginning and they lost no
opportunity to let her know that they were displeased when she received more attention and
tips than both of them. Almost every night somebody came to Skeeter's place solely to see Peggy
and to watch her when she walked across the
room. The sight of her wide eager smile and the
shapely contour of her hips sooner or later cast a
spell over every man who saw her, and most of
them, both married and single alike, proposed
marriage. Peggy consistently refused to consider
the proposals seriously, but she was unable to
conceal the fact that such flattering proposals
were not unwelcome. The other two girls, increasingly resentful of Peggy's popularity, began dou-
ble-dating a customer after hours every night.
However, men continued to come to Skeeter's
place because Peggy was there.

There had been some trouble between Grady

and Skeeter several weeks past. It came about when Skeeter saw Grady give Peggy ten dollars. All three girls took tips, and it was not unusual for a man to give one of them a dollar or two, but ten dollars was unusual. Skeeter had snatched the money from Peggy's hand and thrown it at Grady, telling him to stop trying to buy her favors. Grady had been giving her five- and ten-dollar bills for a long time and he had no intention of stopping as long as he had money to spend, but rather than run the risk of a fight with Skeeter, who always stepped aside at such times and beckoned to Emory Glover, a two-hundred-pound house man and bouncer, he kicked the money in the direction of the two blonde waitresses and walked out of the place. The next time he saw Peggy she told him that Skeeter was angry because she had refused to be his girl and that it would be best not to give her any more tips. After that Grady wadded the money and put it into her hand when no one was looking.

Peggy made another trip to the bar, and when she had served the drinks, she came to Grady's table in the corner. She stood in front of him for several moments, looking down at him questioningly. When he made no response, she sat down quickly beside him.

"What's the matter, Grady?" she asked kindly.

"You're worried about something, aren't you? What is it?"

He turned and looked at her but said nothing.

"You didn't get the money you owe Skeeter, did you?" she said understandingly.

Grady shook his head.

"Oh, Grady, I'm so sorry," she said, looking into his face. "I was afraid you wouldn't be able to get it this soon. You should have had more time."

He nodded slowly.

"I wish there was something I could do, Grady. Would a couple hundred dollars help any? I've got that much saved. You can have it all if you want it, Grady."

"It's twenty-five hundred, Peggy," he said, shaking his head.

"Yes, I know. I heard all about it."

He threw his half-finished cigarette on the floor and stamped it out with his foot.

"Where's Skeeter?"

"I don't know, Grady."

"Has he been here tonight?"

"He left about an hour ago. I heard him tell Emory Glover that he'd be back soon. I don't know where he went."

He felt Peggy's hand come to a rest on his, and he dropped his chin to his chest and looked thoughtfully for a long time at her bright red fingernails.

"Did Skeeter know you'd be here tonight, Grady?"

"Sure, he knew." He laughed shortly. "He told me to be here."

He sat up after that and began fumbling in his pocket for cigarettes. He found the pack, took out a cigarette with shaking fingers, and lit it. When he had finished, he tossed the match stem on the floor.

"There ought to be some way to get next to him," he said, partly to Peggy, partly to himself. He still did not look at her. "He's got a heart in him somewhere—he's bound to have. He couldn't live and breathe unless he had something that passed for a heart. But I'll bet if you stuck a pin in him, he wouldn't even feel it. That tough hide of his would bend a pin, anyway."

"Maybe I could help, Grady."

"How?"

"He wants me to be—to be his girl. He's tried to talk me into that ever since I came here to work for him. That's why he won't let me take more than a dollar tip from anybody. He doesn't want anybody else to have me. If I told him I'd changed my mind——"

"You're crazy!" Grady said roughly. "What do

you take me to be? I wouldn't let you buy him off that way. I may be pretty rotten, but I'm not that far gone."

"But, Grady, I wouldn't mind, if I thought it would do any good. It'd be a lot better for me to do that than it would be to let Skeeter do something awful. You know how he is. He wouldn't stop at anything. He's already told you what he'll do if you don't pay him. Don't you see, Grady? Won't you let me——"

He waved the suggestion away with an impatient sweep of his hand. "No!"

"Please, Grady," she begged. "I'll go to Skeeter and—and talk to him. I'll tell him I've thought it over and that I've changed my mind and that I want to be his girl. When he takes me, I'll tell him I'll like him a lot more if he'll be reasonable and give you enough time to get the money you owe him. He'll have to listen to me. I just know I can do something. Wouldn't that be all right, Grady?"

"Forget it, Peggy," he said. "You're talking about a no-good deal. I won't have any part of that. Here——" He reached into his pocket and took out a crumpled five-dollar bill. After carefully smoothing the paper on the damp table, he handed it to her. "Keep a couple dollars for yourself and then see how far you can stretch the rest of it for

me. I'll start with a couple of drinks right away."
He looked at her, smiling. "And don't spill any
out of the glasses while you're bringing them,
either."

"But, Grady, I don't want the money—not this
time, anyway."

"If I can't trust you to take two dollars, I don't
want to have anything to do with you."

She picked up the five dollars and laid it on her
tray. Then she stood up, smiling and shaking her
head.

"All right, Grady," she said. "There's nobody
else in the world I obey like I do you. You've
really got me going around in circles."

She left and a few minutes later came back
with two drinks of bourbon and a chaser of water
on her tray. She arranged the glasses in a neat
row on the table and sat down. Grady swallowed
the two drinks one after the other. When she
turned and looked at him, she saw that he was
watching her contemplatively.

"What is it, Grady?" she asked.

"I was just thinking about you, Peggy," he said
soberly.

"What do you mean?"

"You're going to make a wonderful wife for
somebody, Peggy. A real bang-up wife. I can tell.
But I'm afraid you're going to get crooked, like

my wife did. That's what always happens to the best girls. They get crooked. I don't know why it is. I crooked my wife, and she didn't deserve it. She's wonderful like you—both of you are wonderful. I'm the dirty dog. I ought to be shot."

"Some things can't be helped, Grady. We all have to take chances."

"Sure. But why do girls like you and my wife take chances on my kind? Looks like you'd know better. I'm no good. Everybody knows that."

"I think I know why she married you, Grady. She loved you, that's why. I'd have done just what she did, if I'd been in her place. You're easy to love, Grady. Too easy. That's the whole trouble. I know."

"If anybody heard us talking like this, they'd think I was trying to talk you into marrying me— or that you were doing the trying." He watched her with a puzzled expression. Peggy lowered her head in order to keep her eyes from meeting his. He reached out and turned her face towards his. She smiled at him self-consciously. "I don't know what to make of it now," he said uncertainly.

They sat in silence for a long time, and finally he found her hand and squeezed it.

"What do you think about that, Peggy?" he asked in hushed tone. "Peggy?"

She shook her head slowly, once more averting

her eyes. "No," she said softly. "I couldn't, Grady. I couldn't do that."

He knocked the empty glasses aside with an angry sweep of his hand. His face was flushed.

"You won't marry me because I'm Grady Dunbar," he said, scowling. "That's it. You've heard all about me. That's the reason."

"Please, Grady, don't talk like that. I like you a lot, but I don't think——"

"You don't have to say it!" he said, speaking out in a loud voice. "I know what you're thinking. You think I'd crook you just like I did my wife. You don't want to take a chance on Grady Dunbar. You've heard too much about him."

There were tears in her eyes when he looked at her. Grady drew a deep breath and slid deep in the seat.

"I like you a lot, Grady—more than you know. I don't want to do anything to hurt you, but——"

"Well, maybe you're right, Peggy." he stopped and laughed to himself. "I'll never amount to a good goddam, no matter how big I talk. I'm glad you're smart enough to know that. It'll save you a lot of headaches."

"Grady," she said imploringly, "please go on back to your wife while you can. It's not too late to do something about it. You'll be a lot happier if you do. I know you will. It's the only way you'll ever be happy. If you'll go back to her and tell her you're sorry, she'll forgive you if you mean it. All you have to do is show her you're really in earnest and, if she's ever loved you, she'll want you back. I'd feel the same way she does if I found out you'd done the kind of things you have, but I'd want you back just the same. I'd forgive you, Grady. She will, too."

"I don't know," he said doubtfully. "It might not work out that way. She's already made up her mind to leave."

"But she'll change her mind, Grady, if you go to her and tell her—tell her that you love her and want her to take you back."

"That sounds good, but it wouldn't work, Peggy. You don't know enough about me. But my wife does. She knows I'm one of the down-and-out aristocracy. The last of the aristocracy, whatever that is. We've petered out. Everybody knows that. When I walk through the front door of the bank, the president ducks out the back door. I couldn't raise a hundred dollars if my life depended on it. Even my cousin, Ben Baxter, even though he's only half-Dunbar, had to go to work practicing law. He makes two dollars every once in a while telling niggers how to borrow twenty-five dollars on a chattel mortgage. That's what we've come down to. There's no future in being a Dunbar."

Peggy suddenly jumped to her feet and he looked up at her inquiringly. She hurriedly began picking up the empty glasses and putting them on her tray. He still did not know the reason for her abruptness until she backed away from the table and enabled him to see Skeeter standing in the doorway between the two rooms. Skeeter was watching him as well as Peggy with a cold penetrating stare.

"I'll have to leave, Grady," she whispered, quickly turning and walking away from him.

When she reached the door, Skeeter was still blocking it and she had to stop. He made her wait several moments before stepping aside and allowing her to continue on her way to the bar in the next room. He had said nothing to her.

Skeeter took his time. He strolled over to the crap table and inspected the game with a series of swift glances. He watched for several minutes and then glanced at Emory Glover. Emory nodded, indicating that the game was going the way it should. When he left the crap table, he glanced around the room, counting the customers.

Ten minutes had passed between the time Skeeter appeared in the doorway and until he walked to the corner where Grady was waiting.

Even after he sat down on the other side of the table, he still did not look directly at Grady, and nothing was said for a long time. The two blonde waitresses hurried to the table. Skeeter nodded briefly towards Grady, and the two girls left. They returned almost immediately with two drinks of bourbon and a chaser of water for Grady. He took one of the drinks at once, slid the empty glass aside, and drew the other glass into his hand.

"I see you got here on time," Skeeter said casually. "That ought to be a good sign."

Grady said nothing, but his shoulders twitched slightly. He continued to turn the whiskey glass around and around in his hand.

"I had a little business to attend to in town tonight," Skeeter said, his eyes watching the room. "If it hadn't been for that, I'd have been here all evening."

Grady raised the glass to his mouth and gulped down the whiskey. His hands were shaking when he set the glass down.

"I'm up against it, Skeeter," he said nervously. "Honest, I am. I couldn't raise the money. I tried every way I could think of. I just couldn't do it, Skeeter."

Skeeter made no reply. There was a long pause. Grady's hands were trembling on the table. He gripped his fingers around the empty glasses in an effort to steady himself.

"You don't know how it is, Skeeter," he said desperately. "When you can't borrow money, there's nothing else you can do."

"Is that so?" Skeeter said, raising the inflection of his voice until it sounded taunting and mocking.

"I've tried hard, Skeeter. The bank won't loan it to me, because there's nothing left to mortgage. I don't know anybody else to go to. My family's down to bedrock. We haven't got a dime."

"What would you do if you'd won twenty-five hundred from me, instead of losing it?"

"Well, I guess I'd want you to pay up."

"Sure, you would! And suppose I wouldn't?"

"I don't know, Skeeter. But I'd want it, anyway."

"Naturally. And you'd make me dig for it, wouldn't you?"

"I guess so."

"Well, that's exactly what I'm telling you to do between now and noon tomorrow. That's twelve hours, and it's the last twelve hours you'll have to do it in. Now, get out and dig for it, or else."

"Else what?"

"What do you think? I don't care how you get

the money as long as you put it in my hand." He shrugged his shoulders indifferently. "Rob a bank. Stick up somebody. Send your wife out to get it. It doesn't matter to me as long as I get what's coming to me. But from now on I'm through begging you, and I'm telling you for the last time."

Grady stood up on shaking knees.

"All right, Skeeter," he said in a husky voice. "I'll do something. I'm going to see Ben Baxter again now."

He saw Skeeter nod his head expressively as he turned and walked out of the smoke-filled room into the cool night air. When he passed the bar, he had not seen Peggy, and he wondered if she were avoiding him purposely.

Chapter XVII

IT WAS SHORTLY AFTER
eight o'clock when Ben Baxter, having been got
out of bed by Grady at a quarter of five that
morning, hurried across the dew-drenched lawn,
entered the square red-brick building with its
towering white columns, ran up the stairway to
the second floor, and walked briskly to the end of
the hall where he paused momentarily for reflec-
tion before opening the door on which was let-
tered JUDICIAL CHAMBERS.

While Ben was standing at the door with his
hand on the knob, several clerks and stenographers
spoke to him as they passed through the hall, but
he was too preoccupied even to hear them, much
less to return their greetings. He had not taken the
time to shave, and his lean face looked grim and
determined in the early morning light.

When Ben finally walked into the room and

closed the door noiselessly behind him, two deputy sheriffs, Mack Poindexter and Stub Pettigrew, and the county recorder, Olin Tharp, were sitting at the big round table with Judge Lovejoy. The unventilated room reeked with the rank odor of stale tobacco smoke. The blinds over the windows had not been opened and the electric-light bulb, which was suspended on a fly-encrusted cord over the table, was still burning. The Negro janitor, Lamar, was leisurely sweeping a litter of cigarette butts and cigar ash into a dust pan. He stopped sweeping when Ben entered, bowing deeply.

"Morning, Mr. Ben," Lamar said pleasantly, leaning one arm on the mantelpiece and the other on the broom handle. "Sure is a fine morning, ain't it, Mr. Ben?"

"Good morning, Lamar," Ben replied, nodding briefly.

"Ah, Mr. Ben!" he said quickly. "Ah, I been aiming to speak to you about a little something, off and on. Ah, I thought maybe you'd be going fishing down on Big Sandy one of these days, and I'd sure like to go along and sort of keep you company, in the background, and drop a line among all them cats myself. Ah, they tell me that the cats sure do bite good these days. Ah, you think maybe I could go along with you, Mr. Ben, and help you with your fishing?"

"I'll let you know the next time I go, Lamar," Ben told him.

"Thank you, Mr. Ben," the Negro said, bowing again.

Ben drew a chair across the room to the table. He sat down slightly behind Judge Lovejoy and leaned forward with his arms resting on his knees.

Judge Lovejoy was a kind-faced white-haired man in his eighties who was always immaculately dressed in striped gray trousers and a black broadcloth coat with a grosgrain piping. He was six feet tall, well preserved for his age, and wore his white whiskers trimmed to a point on his chin. His carriage was stiffly erect and his eyes were always a-twinkle. He had served for almost a quarter of a century as judge of the circuit court, but for the past ten years, since his retirement from the bench, he had engaged in private law practice and, in his soft-spoken but iron-willed manner, had been the absolute and ruthless ruler of county politics. During that time no appointive office had been filled without his approval and no candidate unendorsed by him had ever succeeded at the polls. There were periodic rumblings of dissatisfaction among those who were on the outside, sometimes erupting in outbursts of threats and

revolt against those on the inside, but in his quiet
way Judge Lovejoy always took whatever action
was necessary to insure continued service to the
people. Judge Lovejoy was a bachelor and had
had a room at the Maguffin Hotel for the past
forty years. As far as anyone knew, he had no
living kin. He had come to Maguffin as a young
man, walking the entire distance from the moun-
tains in the northern part of the state. It was said
that the first dollar he had earned in the practice
of law was framed and hanging on the wall of
his bedroom, and that his wealth now amounted
to two or three hundred thousand dollars.

"Raise you two-bits, Tharp," Judge Lovejoy
said in his quiet way, his perpetually kind smile
fixed upon the county recorder. "And I might say
that I'd like to have your considered decision
sometime in the near future."

Olin Tharp screwed up his mouth, wrinkled his
forehead, and fingered the slight stack of white
chips before him on the table. Olin habitually annoyed Judge Lovejoy by studying a weak hand
and a strong hand alike to the same extreme limit.

"Goddam, Olin," Stub Pettigrew said depre-
ciatingly, "he ain't got nothing. I wouldn't be
scared pickled-faced by the Judge if I was you.
He's nothing but a worn-out old bull in a pasture
trying to make the calves think he could raise hell

if he wanted to. The last time I called the Judge, all he had was a puny pair of deuces. Scare the bejesus out of him. Raise the bastard two-bits, Olin."

Olin cut his eyes at Judge Lovejoy and scratched his head thoughtfully.

"That's a lot of money to risk on a little old pot like that one there," Olin said, holding his cards close to his chin and guarding them from sight. "And if you've watched the Judge's game as long as I have, you know he's got them as often as he ain't got them. He don't throw down his cards like other folks, when he gets a weak hand."

"Good God Almighty, Olin," Mack Poindexter said, turning his head a little to one side and spitting tobacco juice in the direction of the spittoon, "don't let the bastard sit there like Jesus Christ on a stump and run you out of the game. What if you do lose a quarter this time? All you have to do is go home and beg another dollar off your old woman and you'll be right back in the game again."

Olin's hands were shaking. Perspiration broke out in beads on his forehead. Judge Lovejoy waited patiently and with the resolute calmness he had acquired in a long lifetime. At the same time his perpetual smile beamed good-naturedly upon Olin's troubled face.

Nate Snoddy, one of the county road commissioners, came in and drew up a chair. He began shuffling the discards while Olin was trying to make up his mind what to do. Nobody spoke to Nate and, as customary, he spoke to no one. The men who dropped in to play a few hands were looked upon as having previously dropped out of the game long enough to sleep or to get a bite to eat. The poker game had been running almost continuously for several years, and practically every lawyer and office-holder in town sat in the game at some time during the day or night.

"By gum, I think I'll take a chance this time," Olin announced with a decisive shake of his head. He carefully placed five white chips in the center of the table. "I'll see you, Judge."

"Goddam!" Stub Pettigrew said in disgust. "Olin, why in hell don't you raise the bastard? If you raised him, he'd drop out if he didn't think he had anything, and you'd win. You'll never get anywhere just by calling the Judge's hand. Ain't you never going to learn nothing!"

"All done, gentlemen?" Judge Lovejoy inquired from behind his ingratiating smile.

"Sure," Mack Poindexter said. "Show your hand, you bastard you!"

Judge Lovejoy laid down his cards, showing four deuces. His radiant smile swept the faces around the table. A prolonged groan came from Stub Pettigrew.

Olin leaned over the table, his mouth agape, and counted the deuces one by one. A miserable expression came to his face.

"I'm a son-of-a-bitch from Atlanta if he ain't got cow teats!" Mack Poindexter said in awe. "Well, what do you know about that!"

Olin turned his cards face down and tossed them to Nate. Judge Lovejoy, his ingratiating smile unchanging, raked in his winnings. He then began stacking his chips in neat rows in front of him.

"I'm through listening to the kind of advice I get around here," Olin said with disgust. He got up, putting his few remaining chips into his pants pocket. "When I come back, I hope I don't find no deputy sheriffs hanging around here. They ought to be out tracking down criminals, anyhow. That's what they draw salaries for. Taxpayers have a right to get something done for all the money they pay out. The people are going to put a stop to it one of these days."

No one said a word while Olin was leaving the room and closing the door, but as soon as he had gone, Mack and Stub let loose roars of laughter. Judge Lovejoy continued to smile benevolently upon one and all alike.

Ben Baxter waited until the deck had been cut and a new hand was being dealt. Then he leaned close to Judge Lovejoy, attracting his attention.

"Judge, I'd like to speak to you for a minute," he said in a low voice. "It's important, Judge."

"What is it about, son?" he responded in his normal tone of voice.

"It's about Grady Dunbar."

"What about Grady?"

"That's what I'd like to speak to you about, Judge," Ben said, still keeping his voice low. "If you'd step out into the hall for just a few minutes——"

"Why, son, we don't do things that way. You know that. Everything that's said in this room is spoken in the utmost confidence, and we respect that. Now, go ahead and tell me what's on your mind, son."

Ben glanced at the men around the table, at the same time drawing his chair a little closer to Judge Lovejoy.

"Grady came to my house before five o'clock this morning, Judge," he said barely above a whisper. "Grady needs money again. He tried to get it at the bank, but that land out there is already mortgaged for the last dollar it's worth. There are already chattel mortgages on the mules and liens on the tractors. The only real property left is the homeplace, and nobody in the county is going to run the risk of having to foreclose on the house during the lifetime of Grady's mother. If she were forced to leave there, the poor farm is the only place she could go."

"How much does Grady Dunbar owe this time, son?" Judge Lovejoy asked, carefully arranging the cards in his hand.

"Twenty-five hundred."

The other men at the table listened with interest. From time to time they glanced at one another, nodding knowingly. Nate Snoddy, sitting on the other side of Judge Lovejoy, nudged him with his elbow.

"It costs a dime to stay, Judge," Nate told him.

The Judge tossed in a red chip.

"Grady Dunbar may be as broke as a nigger on Sunday morning," Mack Poindexter said, cocking his head significantly at Stub and Nate, "but he's got one thing for sure, and that's a hell of a good-looking wife. I'm here to tell you she's really something to bust a button for. I know, because I saw her a couple of times. Good God Almighty, if I had a piece like that around my house, I'd quit this kind of a job and stay home and split lighters or raise rabbits for a living. Great day in the morning! She can give me a peg to hang a hat on anytime she wants to."

"A dime on my two jacks," the Judge spoke up. He tossed two white chips into the pot and leaned back comfortably in his chair.

"My two kings raise you a dime, Judge," Nate said.

Everyone stayed. Ben watched Judge Lovejoy's face, waiting for another opportunity to speak to him.

"You and me both, brother," Stub said, looking up at Mack Poindexter. "But what I'd like to know is, what in hell goes on out there at the Dunbar place. Everybody knows Grady plays around with nigger gals all the time, both out there and here in town. Where does that leave her, huh? You lock the pasture gate on a good-looking woman like her, and something's going to jump the fence, and I don't mean maybe, neither. I've seen it tried before, and it just won't work. These damn fools who marry themselves a good-looking woman and then go off tom-catting from here to hell-and-gone and come back home any old time when they're good and ready and expect to find every little thing exactly like they left it get a hell of a big surprise nearly every time. You can monkey around with a hell of a lot of things in this world, but human nature ain't one of them."

Nate won the pot with his two kings, and Mack began shuffling the cards for a new hand.

"I hate to see Grady in a jam like this, Judge," Ben said uneasily. "I've tried my best to get him to go slow, but you know how headstrong and heedless he is. But even though I've warned him time after time, I still feel that I must help him as long as his mother is alive. It would be a real hardship for his wife and mother if they had to move out of that house, because there's no place they can go. Two innocent women don't deserve to be made to suffer needlessly. That's my real concern in the matter, Judge."

"Son, how long have you been practicing law?" Judge Lovejoy asked, turning and looking at Ben.

"About five years, Judge," he replied. "Why do you ask that?"

The Judge turned back to his cards.

"Because there's a great deal you have yet to learn about your profession, son. Humanitarianism is a commendable endeavor for any man who can afford such indulgence, but it has nothing to do with the practice of law. The same can be said for family ties. Perhaps those are harsh words, but in order to live in this world of ours, you will have to learn to be realistic about realistic matters. Now, when you are ready to discuss the legal aspects of this matter, I will gladly hear you out." He leaned forward and dropped two chips into the pot. "I raise that a dime, Snoddy," he said profoundly.

"Stick with him, Nate," Mack urged. "The bastard's been bulling around here all morning like he's got the only horns in the pasture. It's time somebody cleaned him of every dime he's got. Go on, Nate. Don't be scared of him."

"Are you staying, Mack?" Nate asked with an uneasy tremor in his voice.

"How can I with the kind of mess you deal?" Mack answered, at the same time throwing his cards on the table. "But you're staying, ain't you, Stub?"

"Maybe," Stub said, "But if I do, it'll be because I don't have nowhere else to go."

"Snoddy, have you arrived at your customarily tardy decision yet?" the Judge inquired politely.

"I don't know," Nate said with a shake of his head. "I don't like to do it this early in the morning."

"Hell, you sound just like my old woman, Nate," Mack told him. "Show your manhood if you want to stay in this game."

Sam Weathersbee, the county tax assessor, came in and drew a chair to the table. He slapped Stub on the back, knocking Stub's hat over one eye.

"What's the good word, Mack?" Sam asked casually.

"How much good would it do you if I told you, Sam?"

"I could pass it along, Mack. It might do some of the boys some good, as the fellow said."

"It's been around the world a hell of a lot of times already, and just look at all the trouble it's made!"

"The only time it makes trouble is when it's not handled right. It's all in knowing how, as the fellow said."

"How and when, now and then," Mack droned, swaying his shoulders.

"Why don't you guys dry up?" Stub said. "Can't you see those two shysters there are getting ready to flip heads-or-tails to see which client they're going to hang?"

Nate Snoddy, the road commissioner, lost. He got up and left the room.

"What's the big lawyers' convention about so early in the morning?" Sam Weathersbee asked, nodding at Ben and Judge Lovejoy.

"About Grady Dunbar," Mack told him. "Grady's went and done it again. Ben's been trying to get him off light. The Judge's a mean old son-of-a-bitch, though, and he wants Grady to pay through the nose, or something similar."

"Grady's been gambling again, huh?" Sam said knowingly. "That Grady Dunbar's a damn fool. He'll bet a hundred dollars on the turn of a high card, just like his old man used to do. About two weeks ago I saw him lose eight hundred dollars out at Skeeter's place playing red-and-black. Looks like his wife would make him quit it."

"How do you figure Grady Dunbar's wife could make him quit anything?" Stub asked. "Christ, she can't even get him to start anything."

"For God's sake, she could hold out on him, couldn't she?" Sam said. "My wife's held out on me plenty of times, goddam it!"

"You don't know from nothing, Sam," Stub told him. "He holds out on her. Now, figure that out on your tax-assessing machine."

"You're kidding! You don't mean he holds out on that good-looking——"

"I don't mean Mabel."

Sam looked from one face to the other around the table, his face shining and his eyes sparkling brightly.

"Well, what do you know!" he exclaimed. "For God's sake! What a spot that's going to be for somebody with ambition, as the fellow said! I think maybe I'll make a trip out to that part of the country the first thing next week. A farmer out there in that neighborhood by the name of Haddon has been plaguing me for two years to come out there and give him a lower tax assessment, but I never could be bothered before now. I'm sure glad I remembered about him. By God, I'm going out there next week and scratch around, as the fellow said. Can't no harm come of trying, because it might turn out to be a hell of a good thing."

Stub and Mack looked at each other, nodding in unison. After that, Mack shook his head sadly.

"It never fails, does it, Mack?" Stub said.

"I ain't never known it to fail," Mack agreed. "You let it be known that there's a good spot around somewhere, and before you can pull your shoes on, every half-assed tomcat in town has got his tail up. From now on I'm going to keep my big mouth shut, and the next time I find something, I'm going to hog it first and talk about it afterwards. That's the wise thing to do around this town. I've been cheated out of enough good times to know what to do from now on. I ain't telling nobody nothing after this."

Ben pulled his chair as close as he could to the table and turned his head so he could see Judge Lovejoy's face. The Judge smiled mildly.

"I'd like to come to some understanding with you, Judge," he said earnestly. "If Grady could be given more time, for instance——"

"To whom does Grady owe this money, son?"

"Skeeter Wilhite."

"Why, Wilhite pays me a sizable retainer fee, son," he said in a painful tone. "Wilhite is my client. I'm unalterably obligated to him."

"I know that, Judge. That's why I came to you. I thought we might arrive at some——"

"An attorney, son, a reputable trustworthy attorney, holds his client's interest above any conceivable sentimental considerations. Wilhite has placed his trust and confidence in me. I'm as privy to the man's soul as a priest in a confession box would be. Could I disavow that trust? Could you? Could any attorney who's been steeped in the honorable traditions of the profession? I'm surprised that you would come to me with such an unorthodox proposal. Surely, you are familiar with the ethics of our profession."

"I'm not asking you to disregard Skeeter's interests, Judge. I wouldn't think of such a thing. I'm only asking you to adjust his demands so they'll be more in line with Grady's ability to meet them. Don't you consider that a reasonable request, Judge?"

"Under the circumstances, no!" he said with finality. "I most certainly do not!"

"What circumstances do you mean, Judge?"

Judge Lovejoy turned in his chair until he was looking directly at Ben.

"I prefer not to discuss this or any other legal matter with you or anyone of your ilk, Baxter. My advice to you is to return to your bailiwick."

"I don't understand, Judge," Ben said, puzzled. "What do you mean?"

"You are a nigger-lawyer, Baxter," he said severely. "You've earned that reputation for yourself in the few short years that you've been a member of the bar. I've watched your activities. I know what you've been doing. Every time a nigger with a grudge against a white man comes along you immediately seize him and drag him into your office and begin a crusade against the white race. For instance, take the case of that nigger who works at the saw mill. In spite of your so easily professed friendship for Grady Dunbar, you have encouraged and abetted the nigger to defy Grady's demand that he return to work at the Dunbar place. Moreover, you are conniving with the nigger in an attempt to induce his parents to leave Grady. If you and your nigger-client are successful in this attempt, it will be a damnable precedent, and only a nigger-lawyer would stoop so low. However, son, I'll be perfectly willing to sit down with you and come to some mutually satisfactory agreement concerning this other matter, provided you will assure me that you will take immediate steps to rid yourself of your nigger-clients."

"I couldn't do that, Judge Lovejoy," Ben said uneasily. "No, I couldn't do that."

"Need more be said?" Judge Lovejoy stated as he turned to the game. He beamed at the group around the table. "I have a premonition concerning this particular hand of mine. A nickel it'll be." The chips were thrown in. "I'm especially pleased when I draw a small pair in the beginning, because I find that they often grow and grow and grow." He looked at his hole card with no change of expression. "A dime," he announced. Another card was dealt around. "A magnificent cow from a small calf grows," he concluded.

"You and your cow teats!" Mack Poindexter said in disgust.

The last card was dealt. Stub had a pair of aces showing. Sam Weathersbee had a pair of black eights.

"Two-bits on aces," Stub said matter-of-factly. "Climb aboard if you want to see the sights."

"I can meet that, and raise you two-bits, Pettigrew," Judge Lovejoy stated, throwing his chips on the table. "The longer you ride, the more sights you see."

"What about you, Sam?" Stub asked.

Sam hesitated for several moments before putting his chips into the pot. Mack dropped out. Then it was Stub's turn again.

"Another two-bit raise, friends," he sang out with a joyous lilt. "It's just like the young bride said. The higher you raise it, the better it's going to be for me."

Judge Lovejoy promptly met it and raised another quarter. Sam Weathersbee dropped out with a sigh of relief. Stub began to look uneasy. He studied his cards for a long time, holding them close to his chin. Sweat could be seen popping out on his forehead.

"Maybe that isn't just a lot of bull, Stub," Mack commented, eyeing the Judge. "The old bastard might have something, sure enough."

Stub dug doggedly into his pocket and pulled out a dollar. He threw it on the table and drew out the change.

"That's the third raise," he said grimly. "I could stand three more, considering what I'm holding."

"You'd better be holding your balls and praying for the Judge to drop dead," Sam said. "That's the only chance you've got of winning when the Judge stays for the third raise."

"Suspend the rules, Pettigrew?" Judge Lovejoy asked considerately, a deceptive smile brightening his face. "I'm willing."

Stub shook his head emphatically and drew a deep breath to fortify himself against the inevitable showdown.

"That being the case—" Judge Lovejoy said as he laid down his cards, showing a full house. Stub shook his head sorrowfully at his own three aces.

"One of these days I'm going to clean you like I would a chicken—from your gullet down," Stub told him through gritted teeth. "You and your dad-burn luck!"

Ben scraped his chair in order to attract Judge Lovejoy's attention.

"Judge, if you can't see your way clear to make some sort of concession, I'm afraid we'll have to let this matter go to trial."

"Go to trial!" he said, raising his voice slightly. "I'll be damned if you do! You know good and well my client would have no standing before the court. No court is going to force the collection of a gambling debt in this state. This was a private transaction between two gentlemen. It's a gentleman's transaction, pure and simple."

"You admit, then, that it was an illegal transaction?"

"I admit nothing of the sort!"

"But you decline to make a concession?"

"I most emphatically do!"

Ben stood up and pushed his chair aside. He

looked down upon the snow-white head of the Judge for several moments.

"I suppose you are aware that this is going to bring disaster to Grady," Ben told him coldly.

Judge Lovejoy pushed back his chair and looked up into Ben's face. For the first time that morning he appeared to be kind and fatherly.

"Son, before you leave, I want to offer you some advice. I'm an old man, burdened with prejudices, but there are some things I know to be true. Nothing is to be gained by prolonging the existence of a Grady Dunbar. Let nature take her course, son. I've been watching these old families deteriorate and decay since I was a young man, and I have too much respect for the ways of nature to try to impede her wondrous work. Go on back to your office and help the colored when they come to you for advice. They don't come to me, because they know me. You are young and zealous, and I admire you for what you stand for. We older people say we know how to handle the colored and that we don't want any outside interference, but you know as well as I do that that is our way of trying to cover up our failure. The way to handle the colored is to stop treating them the way Grady Dunbar treats them and let them go to school and get an education and earn their living like the rest of us. There's plenty of room in

this big country for all of us, black and white
alike. You are working against your own ideals,
son, every time you help Grady or anybody else
like him. Now, let nature take her course. The
Dunbars are through as human beings."

Before Ben could speak, Judge Lovejoy waved
him aside and turned his back. The cards were
dealt in silence to the men around the table.
Lamar, leaning on his broom handle, was the only
one who saw Ben walk out of the room. Judge
Lovejoy picked up his cards and studied them
with deep interest.

"A dime is the bet," he said, looking at the faces
around the table. "Do any of you gentlemen happen to be interested to that degree?"

"Count me in, Judge," Sam Weathersbee said
promptly.

They all tossed their chips to the center of the
table and dealing was resumed.

"Say," Mack Poindexter said, looking at Stub,
"maybe me and you'll be going out to the Dunbar place 'most any time now. I didn't think about
that before, but things being the way they are
now, it could happen. I'd give a pretty to get out
there and scratch around before Sam Weathersbee gets there."

Sam smiled to himself and tossed a single white
chip on the table.

"Bet a nickel!" he said.

Chapter XVIII

Late in the afternoon, shortly before sunset, Grady came home drunk. Lucyanne had not expected him back for at least another day, because he had been gone for only twenty-four hours this time, but she knew he was there when a resounding crash jarred the great house. She ran to the window and looked down into the front yard.

As he had often done before, he had driven his car head-on into the brick foundation of the portico. The force of the impact had once more loosened the tall white columns supporting the portico roof, and one of the columns had fallen into the flower bed at the side of the house. Both front fenders were crumpled and the radiator had been mashed flat against the engine. A piece of flying timber had shattered the windshield. Immediately after the crash there was a loud spewing of steam. After several minutes, Grady got out, looked at the wrecked car spellbound, and then kicked the door shut with all his might.

When Grady went up the veranda steps, Lucyanne left the window and stood uncertainly in the center of the room. Presently she could hear him climbing the stairway, and she ran to the door and locked it. As she had expected, he came up the hall, yelling for her at the top of his voice, and was soon kicking the door.

"Lucyannie! Where are you, Lucyannie?"

She trembled for a long fearful moment when she heard him trying to insert a key into the lock. The key failed to open the door, however, and he began kicking it again.

"I know you're in there, Lucyannie!" he shouted at her. "You can't hide from me! I always know how to find you!"

He tried to break down the door by throwing his weight against it. The wooden panels creaked under the strain.

"If you don't open this door, I'll get an axe and chop it down, Lucyannie!"

"Please don't, Grady!" she cried. "You mustn't do that! What do you want?"

"I want a drink," he said after a pause, his voice tempered with a pleading supplication. "You'll do that for me, won't you, Lucyannie?"

"Oh Grady!" she said, unable to keep from feeling sorry for him. "You know I don't have any whiskey."

"Would you give it to me if you had it, Lucyannie? You'd do that for old times' sake, wouldn't you, Lucyannie? You wouldn't tell me a lie, would you?"

"Oh Grady, you know I'd give it to you if I had it!"

"I thought so," he said. His voice had become friendly and subdued. "I knew you'd do a little thing like that for me if you could. You've always been good to me. You're not the kind to hold a grudge against a fellow, are you, Lucyannie?"

"No, Grady."

"If I learned some sense, things might be different around here, mightn't they, Lucyannie?"

"Yes, Grady."

"I've been thinking about that all day," he said earnestly. "I should've been thinking about it a lot sooner than this, though. It might be too late now."

"It's not too late if you really make up your mind to do it, Grady."

"I don't know," he said doubtfully. "Things have gone pretty far now."

He was quiet for several minutes after that, and Lucyanne thought he had gone down the hall to his room. She was startled when she heard him suddenly knock on the door.

"What is it, Grady?" she asked anxiously.

"I'm sorry I bothered you, Lucyannie," he told her.

After that she heard him moving unsteadily down the hall. He went to his room and closed the door. There were tears in her eyes when she turned and went to the daybed. In spite of all she could do, she found herself crying miserably. She told herself over and over that if she had not locked her door, everything might have turned out differently.

A quarter of an hour had passed when she heard Grady running up the hall. He was soon knocking urgently on the door, and she had to force herself not to go near it. She knew what could happen if she opened the door now.

"Lucyannie?" he called to her.

"Yes, Grady?"

"I forgot to tell you something."

"What is it?"

She could feel a painful pounding in her breast while she held her breath and waited to hear what he was going to say.

"I didn't get the money to pay him."

"Oh!" she exclaimed nervously. "You didn't?"

"No."

She could not think of anything to say that would let him know how she felt, but she wanted desperately to tell him something that would express her concern and disappointment.

"You know what I'm talking about, don't you, Lucyannie?" he asked.

"Yes, Grady, I know. I'm awfully sorry. I wish——"

She had to stop in order to keep her voice under control. Her hands felt limp and weak when she tried to grip her fingers on the back of a chair.

"Ben Baxter talked to Judge Lovejoy about it, and nothing much came of it. Then Ben went to see Skeeter and tried to get him to wait until I could sell the cotton crop this fall, but Skeeter wouldn't listen. I guess there's no way out of it, Lucyannie. Ben's done everything he can, and there's nobody else I can go to."

"But, Grady, what are you going to do!"

"I don't know," he said in a helpless manner. "I don't know what to do."

"Grady, I'd help you any way I could," she told him. "You know that, don't you?"

He made some reply, but his words were indistinct, and the sound of his voice trailed off as he turned away from the door.

She could hear every sound he made as he

walked heavily down the hall to his room and closed the door. For the next half-hour she sat tensely on the edge of her bed, listening for some sound in his room. The one thought that raced through her mind was that she might be able to persuade Skeeter to be reasonable if she went to him herself and talked to him. She had no idea what she would say or do, but she felt that she had to make an effort to accomplish something before it was too late. While she sat there thinking confusedly, she heard a car come up the lane at a rapid rate of speed and squeak to a stop in the driveway. Right away the horn began blowing in loud persistent blasts. She went to the window, but it was already growing dark, and she could not recognize the car.

Grady left his room and went down the stairs to the front veranda. She could see him move unsteadily across the white sandy yard to the car. When he got there, he fell drunkenly against the side of it. Skeeter Wilhite opened the door and stepped to the ground.

Their voices suddenly became loud and angry, but she could not understand what either was saying. The belligerent argument grew in intensity until both were shouting. Then Grady lunged at Skeeter, striking at him with his fist, but Skeeter stepped aside and Grady fell headlong on the ground. He got up, shouting curses at Skeeter. When Lucyanne saw Skeeter shove Grady backwards until he fell against the side of the automobile, she knew she had to try to do something right away. She ran out of the room and down the stairway to the veranda.

Just as she started down the veranda steps she saw both of them draw pistols and begin shooting. She cried out, but her voice was lost in the sound of pistol-fire. Grady was the first to move. His hands dropped to his sides, the revolver fell from his fingers, and he sank to the ground. Taking deliberate aim, Skeeter fired two more bullets into Grady's body. He looked down at Grady for a moment and then ran to his car. Crying frantically, Lucyanne ran across the yard but, before she could reach him, the car was already moving rapidly out of the driveway. The headlights were switched on and the car roared down the lane.

She fell on her knees beside Grady and lifted his head with her arms. Her eyes were blinded with tears and she had to wipe them away before she could see him clearly.

"Grady! Grady!" she cried brokenly.

He opened his eyes and looked up into her face. A smile, almost indiscernible in the faint light, came to his lips as he recognized her.

"Oh, Grady, why did this have to happen?" she said tenderly. "Why did it—why did it!"

Tears filled her eyes again and she had to wipe them away with the back of her hand.

"It didn't turn out very good, did it, Lucy-annie?" he said weakly. "You got the worse of the bargain. It should never've been that way."

"Don't say that, Grady." She held him close in her arms. "You mustn't feel like that."

"That doesn't matter. I know it was a bad bargain for you, Lucyannie. I didn't do you right. It's all my fault. I'm sorry now, but it's too late to help any. If I had a chance all over again, I'd try—but I don't know if I could do any better next time. I guess it wasn't in me to treat you right. I wanted to, but it just wouldn't come out."

"Oh, Grady, I've always loved you, no matter what happened. I couldn't help it. I've always known I'd love you as long as you lived——"

She caught her breath sharply when she realized what she had said and hugged him tightly in her arms.

"Don't think too hard of me, Lucyannie," he said slowly, the words forming weakly on his lips. "I used to try hard, but I couldn't do anything about it. I guess I was made to be like I am."

He was becoming weaker all the time. Holding him tenderly in her arms, she wanted to say something, anything, that would comfort him, but her throat was choked and her lips were useless when she tried to move them.

"Lucyannie——"

She bent over him, looking down into his eyes. "What is it, Grady? Tell me!"

"Lucyannie . . . think of me sometimes. . . ."

She could feel an unexpected heaviness of his body. She quickly squeezed him into her arms while tears dropped on his pale quiet face.

There was the sound of many feet running on the hard white sand, and when she looked around, she could see flickering shadows and lantern light all around her.

"Miss Lucyanne, my goodness me, what awful thing has happened?"

She recognized Martha's frightened voice. Martha, Uncle Jeff Davis, Pete, and five or six other Negroes from the quarter stood in the lantern light. The headlights of an automobile flashed upon them as a car came up the lane and came to a quick stop in the driveway.

"Oh Lordy, help us now!" Martha wailed as she looked at Grady's body on the ground. She dropped on her knees beside Lucyanne. "Oh Lordy, oh Lordy, help us now!"

Ben Baxter got out of the car and ran to them.

"Lucyanne!" he said, out of breath. He got

down beside her. "I got here as quick as I could," he told her. "As soon as I heard that Skeeter had left town and driven out in this direction, I came out here as fast as I could. I was afraid something like this was going to happen."

They heard a commotion in the hallway and looked around just as Mama Elsie ran to the veranda. Ben jumped up and hurried to the steps to prevent her from coming out into the yard where Grady's body lay but, before he could reach her, her huge body fell heavily on the floor. As soon as she realized what had happened, Lucyanne ran to her.

Ben caught her at the steps. "It's too late now, Lucyanne," he said, shaking his head. "It was the sudden excitement and the exertion of running through the house. It was more than her heart could stand."

Ben motioned to the Negro men and they carried Mama Elsie's body back into the house and placed it on the sofa in the parlor. When they came back to the yard, Will Harrison and Brad were just getting out of the truck.

"We heard the shots and then saw a car drive off in a big hurry," Will told Ben. "I knew right away something had gone wrong up here."

Brad watched Lucyanne and Ben. "Who killed Grady?" he asked after a while.

"Skeeter Wilhite was here," Ben told him.

Brad looked at him closely.

"What are you doing here?"

Ben glanced at him in surprise but said nothing.

"I said for sure when I heard those shots, that Skeeter Wilhite was up here," Will said. "It was bound to happen sooner or later. Both of them, Grady and Skeeter, are the kind to settle things with a gun when things go wrong. I just knew something like that was going to break out between them. It couldn't fail, knowing them both like I do."

Will started towards the house.

"I don't reckon it will help none to call the doctor now," he said, "but I'll phone him, anyway. Somebody ought to notify the sheriff right away, and I'll do that, too."

After Will had gone into the house, Ben walked over to where Uncle Jeff Davis was standing in the group of Negroes.

"Everything will be taken care of here after a few days, Uncle Jeff Davis," Ben told him, "and after that you and your wife can move to town. You can tell everybody else in the quarter they can leave, too."

"Thank you, sir, Mr. Ben," the old Negro said

solemnly as tears filled his eyes. "I sure do thank you, sir, Mr. Ben."

As Ben turned around to go to Lucyanne, he found himself face to face with Brad.

"What do you think you're doing?" Brad said angrily. "Who said you could run things around here?"

"I don't know what you mean," Ben told him. "Somebody has to help out here. Lucyanne needs help at a time like this——"

"You're not going to take her away from me!" Brad said, stepping back and raising his fists.

Lucyanne ran to Ben, clutching his arm. Ben looked down at her, puzzled and perplexed.

"I don't understand, Lucyanne," Ben said to her. He looked at her searchingly. "Do you want me to leave?"

She quickly shook her head and, turning from Brad, pressed her face against him.

Brad, breathing heavily, watched them with rising resentment. His face was flushed with anger.

"I'm not good enough for you, am I?" he said in a taunting outburst of emotion. "You won't have anything to do with me because I'm a low-white! I should've known it! You're just like all the rest of them. You had me fooled, because I thought you were different. But you're not! You're

just like any Dunbar!" He walked part way across
the yard. "Go on and stay with your kind. But
one of these days you'll wish you'd taken up with
me when you had the chance."

Turning his back, he went off into the night.
The evening breeze from the low country began
rustling the leaves of the red oaks once again and
over the upland slope was spread the pungent
odor of burning pine.